ALSO BY SHELDON COHEN

STORY OF THE JEW

SHELDON COHEN

authorHOUSE®

AuthorHouse™
1663 Liberty Drive
Bloomington, IN 47403
www.authorhouse.com
Phone: 1 (800) 839-8640

Scripture quotations marked KJV are from the Holy Bible, King James Version
(Authorized Version). First published in 1611. Quoted from the KJV Classic
Reference Bible, Copyright © 1983 by The Zondervan Corporation.

Published by AuthorHouse 12/18/2017

ISBN: 978-1-5462-2157-9 (sc)
ISBN: 978-1-5462-2156-2 (e)

Library of Congress Control Number: 2017919103

Print information available on the last page.

Any people depicted in stock imagery provided by Thinkstock are models,
and such images are being used for illustrative purposes only.
Certain stock imagery © Thinkstock.

This book is printed on acid-free paper.

AUTHOR BIOGRAPHY

Sheldon Cohen has practiced Internal Medicine for forty years, and served as a medical director of a Chicago suburban hospital and two Health Maintenance Organizations. As a member of the Joint Commission on Accreditation of Healthcare Organizations, he served as a quality consultant for hospitals in the United States, South America, Europe, and consulted with the Ukraine Ministry of Health for the development of a nationwide hospital accrediting body.

The author, as his name implies, is a Jew with an intense interest in Jewish history.

I dedicate this book to

BETTY LOU
Gail, Paul,
Amanda, Shane, Megan, Travis, Carly, Alexa, Ethan, Emily,
Derek, Rylie, Benjamin

CONTENTS

INTRODUCTION

There are many books on the subject of Jewish history. Nevertheless, I decided to write another one because I love to write, and I find writing to be the best way to learn and assist in keeping one's brain alive and functioning. Also, as regards the subject of this book, I am a Jew, and my family members as far back as the 1800s were all Jewish. They lived in Poland under Russian dominance until 1904 when they "fled the Czar" and arrived by boat to America. They left their ancestral homeland because Jews were being persecuted: as a young child, my maternal grandmother witnessed an elderly Jew being beheaded by a sword-wielding "cossack" on horseback; my maternal grandfather faced persecution as a Jew in the Russian army. He deserted, but was quickly captured. The penalty for desertion was death, but his Russian guard was quoted as saying, "Let the young man go. His family is already in America." My future maternal grandfather was one very lucky man—and I became the future recipient of two more aunts and one uncle and six cousins.

My paternal grandfather was a Kohan (a hereditary honor passed down to all male descendants from the ancient temple high priests of biblical times). This "honor" gave me, as a Bar Mitzvah youngster and the only Kohan in the synagogue on Richmond Street in Chicago, the privilege of making a special prayer for the congregation; a prayer which was so profound that I had to be covered with a large prayer shawl concealing my face, lest any of the congregants who happened to catch a glimpse of my face while I was praying would instantly be struck dead—or so I was told. My hands had to be in a certain position: the back of my hands in front of my face with tips of thumbs touching, the other four fingers of each hand separated into doublets, and the large shawl stretching over my head to cover my face by reaching over my outstretched finger tips.

So there I was, standing on an elevated stage before the congregation chanting the special prayer when one of my class mates walked below me and looked up under my shawl directly into my face before passing out of my view. When I finished and descended from the stage, he came up to me, smiled and said, "I looked right in your face, and I'm still alive." I have never forgotten the interesting experience that day.

Let's get on with our four thousand years old, and as yet unfinished, amazing story of the evolution of the world's first religion—Judaism.

PART ONE

FROM ADAM AND EVE TO 1 BCE

IN THE BEGINNING

With that "modern day" story behind us, let us go on to Judaism's origins. A rabbi named Yossi ben Halafta, active in the second century, suggested that Judaism's origins started with Adam and Eve. If true, it behooves us to dissect this era. If you believe in Adam and Eve, then you believe that they were created by God in the Garden of Eden. According to Wikipedia, a 2014 poll reports that 56% of Americans believe that Adam and Eve existed.

The biblical story of Adam and Eve goes something like this: God made Adam by shaping a humanoid figure from "ground clay;" another version speaks of "dust of the earth." When His creation was formed to His liking, God breathed into the shape. Adam's eyes opened. God placed Adam in a beautiful garden named Eden and gave him the responsibility to look after this new world which God filled with animal and plant life of all kinds. Then he realized that Adam needed a companion, so he made a woman out of one of Adam's ribs. He named her Eve.

Adam and Eve were happy in each other's company. God gave them the caretaker role of their new home. He blessed them and told them that it was their responsibility to look after their beautiful new surroundings. He also gave them one warning, "All of this is yours to sustain and care for. Never touch that single beautiful tree in the center of the garden. It gives knowledge of good and evil and if you eat of its fruit you will lose immortality, and death will be your lot." Apparently, God wanted them to know only about "good" and not "evil."

They followed this rule until, one day, a serpent in the garden spoke with them. He asked if God told them they could eat the fruit growing within the Garden. Eve answered, "Yes, but not from the tree in the center which God said was the Tree of Good and Evil."

"How silly," said the serpent, "Eating of The Tree of the Knowledge of Good and Evil will teach you what is right and wrong, and do you not believe that you should have that right?" Here we see the first temptation affecting mankind.

The attractiveness of the fruit on the tree and the thought that Adam and eve would now be able to discern right and wrong made them both partake of the fruit. But once they did, they started to feel that they had done something wrong, and they became fearful of God. As it turned out, God lamented the fact that Adam and Eve disobeyed Him. He ordered them out of the Garden telling them that they were on their own now, would have to sustain themselves by their own efforts, will experience pain during childbirth, and be subjected to an inevitable death.

So, this Adam and Eve theory of the origin of man on earth remains to this day, and, as mentioned before is accepted by 56 percent of humanity.

Those who do not accept that Adam and Eve tell the story of the beginning of man on earth have to rely on an alternate theory which states that mankind evolved in a slow evolutionary process for which there is considerable, but perhaps conflicting evidence. This theory suggests that human life evolved, along with apes, from an apelike ancestor of antiquity along two different evolutionary pathways—animal (primate) and man.

Charles Darwin championed these theories in his famous The Origin of the Species (1859), written while sailing around the world for five years aboard his famous HMS Beagle in the 1830s. He postulated that man has, from time immemorial, continued to pass on mutations via the genetic sequence. These mutations result from reproductive errors and various environmental changes brought on by radiation or chemicals. In the natural selection process, the fittest members of a species are able to pass on their genetic information while the unfit die off. This all occurs over millions of years.

So, what we have are two alternate theories of how man multiplied and populated the earth: one, via Adam and Eve, and two, via Darwinian natural selection. Take your pick.

What does all this have to do with Judaism? As man evolved by whatever route you choose, and as intellectually they developed increasing capacity to think, the concept of religion entered their minds which they championed and promoted over time. They needed this development perhaps because of the snake that caused Adam and Eve to bite that apple resulting in evil, as well as good, now permeating the earth. I leave it to the reader to decide if religious development was a good trend. In support of the thesis that it was a good trend, and from the standpoint of the development of a moral code over time with rules of behavior, necessary because there were none, it clearly evolved from moral thinkers of the primitive evolving ancient communities who had to fight for their beliefs against unbelievable odds. Multiple religions did indeed become established eventually, but the religious wars, which ensued throughout history, added a negative element to the argument between good and bad. Anyhow, now there are religions entrenched in our world. Why was it necessary? Let us see how and why they evolved. Who were its moral and ethical pioneers?

NOAH

Noah was tenth in the line of ascendancy from Adam. God noted that Noah was one of the righteous in a world of evil. So much so that God states that man was evil and redemption was not an option. The evil had risen to a point that God says in **Genesis 6:5** *The Lord saw that the wickedness of man was great in the earth, and that every intention of the thoughts of his heart was only evil continually.*

God decided to rectify this evil by destroying human life on earth. He would cause a great flood to engulf the earth, but at the same time would save Noah and his family by causing them to build an ark within which they would bring pairs of animals who would inhabit the earth. Noah would become heir to the good life that comes with a life of righteousness and pass it on ad-infinitum to all of future humanity. It was a moral teaching God would impress upon the world: one could be righteous and thrive, or unrighteous and die. The life of Noah was to be used as a lesson from which mankind could learn that the path of righteousness was the path to a good life—hopefully the future pioneers of religious thought would understand as they developed their precepts of religion—but would they?

THE START

As regards the history of religious development, there are some ancient forms of worship known as shamanism, and animism. Shamanism involves practitioners who become trancelike, and while in this state practice divination and healing; predicting future events. Animism practitioners believe natural phenomena and objects, even including the universe, possess souls. These two "religions" date back 300,000 years BCE.

Religions did flourish over time. This was all in an effort of humankind to develop a moral code—a code to rules of behavior and relationships between an increasing number of diverse human beings; people only interested in asserting their own authority come hell or high water. Religion evolved in an effort to change this mind-set. This evolution is a daunting task whose success or failure remains controversial even 4000 years after its original thought.

Older religions that are still practiced today are Buddhism, Hinduism, Jainism, Taoism, and the first one: Judaism. Their sites of origin are: Buddhism in Nepal, Hinduism in India, Janism in Nepal, Taoism in China, and Judaism in an area now known as Israel. Before we zero in on the first religion, Judaism, the subject of this book, we will introduce the first four briefly.

Buddhism evolved from the mind of Siddhartha Guatama, a prince of a Nepalese tribe. Nepal is a landlocked Himalayan country. In approximately 560 BCE, at the age of 29, Guatama left his home, took years of Yoga training, studied the extensive suffering he felt was rampant in the world, meditated, and eventually became a Buddha, or enlightened one, who founded the religion of Buddhism. Its five main principles are:

1. Never take a life of anything living.
2. Only take something freely given.
3. Never engage in sexual misconduct.
4. Never lie.
5. Never lose mindfulness (keep the mind intact to deal with problems by avoiding any form of intoxication that impairs rational and ethical thought processes).

There are 300,000,000 Buddhists world-wide.

Hinduism evolved over time with no single founder or group of individuals given credit for its development. There are one billion adherents making it the third largest religion in the world after Christianity and Islam (more on these last two later).

Hinduism has four tenets

1. Pursue prosperity through hard work, and also perform civic and governmental service.
2. Pursue exercise and passion, but not hedonistically.
3. Pursue scholarship through study and meditation.
4. Live in cooperation with your fellow humans.

Jainism is an offshoot of Hinduism and Buddhism. Originating in India, it has a small number of adherents numbering 4,000,000. It does not believe in a Creator God, but rather accepts the universe as an aspect of matter. They believe in Ahimsa which means that one's spirit, body, and mind cannot possibly think violently. It was this philosophy that supported Ghandi in his efforts to free India from Great Britain.

Taoism Principally in China where there are only 2.7 million adherents. The smallness of their numbers, in comparison to their population of more than a billion, is understandable in a Communist country where religion has been deemphasized. Adherents believe in a sovereign divinity, a heaven, and venerate their ancestors whom they worship.

ORIGIN OF THE JEW

Before we get to a discussion about Judaism's history over time, it should be known that the current world population totals 7.5 billion. If one couples this with the Jewish world population of 14.5 million, it means that Jews represent 0.53 percent of the world's total population. The United States and Israel combined constitute 83 percent of the Jewish world population, and the remaining 17 percent are scattered in 98 other countries. Israel is the only country in the world with a Jewish majority.

It was more than 100 years ago when Mark Twain was quoted as follows: *"if the statistics are right, the Jews constitute but one percent of the human race. It suggests a nebulous dim puff of smoke lost in the blaze of the Milky Way. Properly the Jew ought hardly to be heard of; but he is heard of, has always been heard of. He is as prominent on the planet as any other people, and his commercial importance is extravagantly out of proportion to the smallness of his bulk. His contribution to the world's list of great names in literature, science, art, music, finance, medicine, and abstruse learning, are also way out of proportion to the weakness of his numbers. He has made a marvelous fight in this world, and has done it with his hands tied behind him. All things are mortal but the Jew; all other forces pass, but he remains. What is the secret of his immortality?"* Remember, this comment was written in more modern times.

Unbeknownst to a youngster named Abram, he would be considered the conceiver of a religion that gradually, in the distant future, would come to be known as Judaism. When he commenced his activities, which over much time would evolve into the Jewish religion with its adherents known as Jews, he was a young boy confused by what he considered the irrational activity of his father. Abram (his future name would be Abraham) was born in Ur, Babylonia. His father was Terach, an idol merchant, who sold idols to the citizens so that they could worship and pray to them. This was anathema to young Abram who considered that idol worship was ridiculous. He would teach his father a lesson. He smashed all the idols with a hammer except for the largest one, and then placed the hammer in the hands of the largest idol. As the story has been told, when Abram's father returned he was aghast at what happened and asked for an explanation from his son. Abram calmly answered that "the idols all got into a fight and the largest one smashed the smaller ones." Abram's father answered incredulously that Idols can't do that. "Then why do you worship them?" answered Abram.

God must have gotten wind of this advanced thinking of the time, because he called to Abram and asked if he would leave his home and family, and go on the road acting as God's messenger to make a great nation in God's name.

It was an offer Abram could not refuse. He travelled through what is now known as the land of Israel for many years. He married Sarai. His ambition and drive to excel was a trait that he would instill in Jews of the future. God promised Abram that he would make of him and his wife, Sarai, a great nation. But to this point in time, Sarai, Abram's wife, was infertile; no children emanated from the marriage.

Sarai had an Egyptian handmaiden named Hagar who was a helper to Sarai in managing affairs of the family. This time in history, and in accordance with legal codes of the time, it was not considered unusual for a barren wife to suggest that her husband impregnate another woman whose child would belong to the barren wife and her husband. This was a way of a barren woman acquiring a child. Abram agreed.

Genesis 16:3 states *"And Sarai, Abram's wife, took Hagar, her Egyptian maid, and gave her to her husband Abram to be his wife."* **Genesis 16:4 states** *"And he went into Hagar, and she conceived: and when she saw that she had conceived, her mistress was despised in her eyes."* Sarai, of course, recognized what had happened. Tension reigned supreme in the household. Nothing but trouble would be the future consequence for the world from this point on.

Genesis 16:5 states *"And Sarai said unto Abram, My wrong be upon thee. I have given my maid into thy bosom, and when she saw that she had conceived I was despised in her eyes. The Lord judge between me and thee."* In essence, Sarai was asking her husband Abram to solve this dilemma. **Genesis 16:6** states, but Abram said unto Sarai, *"Behold, thy maid is in thy hand; do to her as it pleaseth thee."* In essence, Abram turned the problem back to Sarai, who did indeed take control. She dealt harshly with Hagar who *"fled from her face."* And the angel of the LORD found Hagar nearly dying of thirst in the desert and saved her by giving her water. **Genesis 16.8** And he said, *"Hagar, Sarai's maid, whence camest thou? And wither wilt thou go?" And she said, "I flee from the face of my mistress Sarai."* And the angel suggested that she was putting her life at risk in the hot desert and she should go back to her mistress and continue under her service. **Genesis 16:9** *And the angel of the LORD said unto her, "Return to thy mistress, and submit thyself under her hands."*

Now recognizing her risk, Hagar did indeed agree to return. **Genesis 16:10** *And the angel of the LORD said unto her, "I will multiply thy seed exceedingly, that it shall not be numbered for multitude."* Hagar gave birth to a son. He was named, Ishmael.

When Abram was 99 years of age and Ishmael was 13, God returned to Abram's home. He promised Abram descendants through Sarai in spite of their age, and changed their names to Abraham and Sarah. In addition, he told Abraham that he "would be the father of many nations," and promised him the land of Canaan, on the Mediterranean coast encompassing what is now northern Israel and Lebanon on the western border of modern day Syria. God added, *"I will be your God."* In addition he advised Abraham that all of his descendants, in order to be identified, would require the ritual of circumcision. Here we see the first anatomical rule of the fledgling Jewish religion.

Sarah, in spite of her advanced age, would have a son named Isaac. Isaac, along with Ishmael would be the originator of two dynasties: Ishmael… the Arab nations. Isaac…Judaism. From that time to the present day, the relationship of Isaac's and Ishmael's descendants would, unfortunately, never be fully conducive to close friendship.

Genesis 23 *Sarah lived to be a hundred and twenty-seven years old. She died at Kiriath Arba (that is, Hebron) in the land of Canaan, and Abraham went to mourn for Sarah and to weep over her.*

Abraham died at the age of 175. His legacy would be all future Jews of the world. The time of Abraham is considered to have begun approximately 1812 BCE. God is said to have chosen Abraham and his descendants from his son, Isaac, to create a nation as an example of the good that can ensue for humanity. He gave Abraham and his progeny land that was intended to evolve into an example for the world to follow.

THE FIRST JEWS

Once Isaac (son of Sarah) was born, he became first in the lineage of Abraham as opposed to Ishmael (son of Hagar). God apparently tested Abraham; he ordered Abraham to sacrifice his son Isaac to prove his loyalty to God, a violent act which Abraham was about to carry out, but God prevented Abraham at the last minute once God had seen Abraham's dedication.

When Isaac was forty years old and still unmarried, Abraham decided to find his son a bride. He did not want Isaac to marry one of the local Canaanite women, so he sent Eliezer, a servant, to Mesopotamia to bring back a suitable wife for Isaac. Eliezer accomplished this task by bringing back Rebecca after she had passed suitable verbal tests. The union of Isaac and Rebecca produced twins, but not until twenty years later when Isaac was sixty and prayed to God for Rebecca to become pregnant and produce a child. She did better than that—she produced Esau and Jacob. Esau would evolve into an outdoors-man hunter and his father Isaac's favorite, while a more intellectual Jacob would become his mother Rebecca's favorite.

Esau married when he was forty years of age. His two wives, Judith and Basemath, were Hittite women, despised by Isaac and Rebecca. When Isaac was elderly and had grown blind, he asked Esau to prepare a meal for him at which time he would give him a blessing before God would take him. Isaac's wife Rebecca heard Isaac's discussion with Esau and she told Jacob to disguise himself as Esau by wearing goat skin to mimic Esau who was a very hairy man, so that Jacob would receive Isaac's blessing. When Esau discovered Jacob's trick, he vowed to kill him, but Rebecca, fearful for Jacob's life, sent him away to "take a wife from the daughters of my brother Laban."

Time would pass and Rebecca died and was buried in the cave of Machpelah, an ancient Jewish site, the second holiest Jewish site next to the Temple Mount, and the same burial ground of Abraham, Sarah, and Isaac, who died at the age of 180—all forever to be identified as the founders of a religion known as Judaism.

JOSEPH 11TH SON OF JACOB

Joseph, the eleventh son of Jacob, was his father's favorite. This did not sit well with Joseph's older brothers, so they hatched a plot to get their younger brother out of their lives, especially when their father presented Joseph with a multicolored coat. Their jealousy knew no bounds. They viewed their younger brother as a boaster, especially as Joseph began to suggest that he would someday be the family ruler. The resentment this fostered in his older brothers caused them to desire to do away with Joseph, so they hatched a plot to kill him in the surrounding wilderness. This remedy, however was protested by Reuben, the eldest brother, so instead of a death sentence, Joseph is sold by his brothers as a slave to a prominent Egyptian named Potiphar, while at the same time they lied to their father, Jacob, telling him that Joseph was slain by wild beasts, prompting Jacob to enter into an extended mourning.

In the meantime, Potiphar assigned Joseph some household duties, and when he sees the superb work ethic of Joseph he makes him supervisor of his household. This excellent progress, however, is interrupted by Potiphar's wife who attempts to seduce Joseph. When Joseph rebuffs her attempt she accuses Joseph of rape, and he ends up imprisoned. There Joseph is asked for an interpretation of one of his fellow prisoner's dream, and Joseph's interpretation proves to be right on the mark. This prisoner, once freed from prison, goes back to work for the Egyptian King, and in the future advises the king of Joseph's amazing interpretation gifts. When the king is in urgent need of advice relative to agricultural problems, Joseph is able to predict seven years of excellent harvests followed by seven years of famine, which Joseph prevented when he suggested that they needed to save grain during the plentiful grain years to be prepared for the drought years. Joseph's brilliant ability to foretell the future earns him a job second only in importance to the king of Egypt.

Even Canaan feels the sting of the grain shortage, so Jacob sent his ten sons to Egypt in order to buy grain. There they meet their long lost brother Joseph, but they do not recognize him. Joseph then reveals his true identity, and in an act of great compassion forgives them all. We see here the contrast between Joseph who carries religious precepts and his brothers who do not. Jacob and his family move to Egypt. Joseph has exercised mercy in relation to his bothers.

Genesis 45.5 "*And now do not be distressed or angry with yourselves because you sold me here, for God sent me before you to preserve life*".

Joseph's life followed religious precepts. As opposed to his brothers, he never forgot those precepts. He was perfect to be in the line of those who founded religion, and in this case, what would turn out to be the Jewish religion. He would not turn his back on God even though circumstances would lead one to believe he was being abandoned by God. "*The Lord was with Joseph so that he prospered—and Joseph was with the Lord*". When circumstances turn you in the wrong direction, think right and never abandon God's precepts.

Joseph knew these precepts and it kept him in good stead: he never lost trust in God. He followed God's precepts rather than be negatively affected by adverse circumstances. He never lost integrity. He had humility and knew the virtue of forgiveness. He never understood hatred and was always quick to forgive.

In short, Joseph played a vital role in passing on the concept of religion and was a perfect disciple, well fitted to enter the chain of the developers of religious precepts.

MOSES

Born in Egypt during the 400 year period of exile, Moses was the youngest of three children of Amram and Jochebed. He had an older brother and sister, Miriam and Aaron. His birth year was 1391or 2 BCE. These exiled Jews (Israelites or Hebrews) eventually became slaves under a Pharoah who, fearful of their accelerating birth rate, ordered that all new born Hebrew males were to be drowned in the Nile River. In those days apparently rulers were deified and could commit heinous crimes anytime without fear of punishment; another important reason for a religious evolution for the world.

Jochebed hid her newborn son, Moses, during the first three months of his life after which she placed him in a basket and floated him down the Nile. Moses sister, Miriam, kept careful watch on his progress which was interrupted by Pharoah's daughter, Bithiah, who heard Moses crying. Barren herself, she kept Moses as her own. Based upon the intervention of Miriam, Bithiah made Moses mother, Jochebed, the infant's wet nurse. Moses would thrive amongst Egyptian royalty and received a superb education. Somehow he learned about his Hebrew origin, and slowly he developed sympathy for his people who were forced to do slave labor.

When Moses witnesses an Egyptian enforcer beating a Hebrew to death, he lost control and killed him. Although Moses thought that no one had seen him, that turned out not to be the case.

One of the protagonists who saw Moses in his deadly act asked if Moses intended to kill him just as he had killed the Egyptian enforcer. Moses' secret was not a secret! If the Pharoah found out, Moses could be in great danger, so he fled Egypt and arrived at Midian where he came across seven young women watering their flock arguing with shepherds who were trying to drive the girls away. Moses drove the shepherds away and became friends with one of the girl's father, Jethro. While tending Jethro's flock, Moses came across a burning bush from which emanated a voice telling him to remove his shoes as he was standing on holy ground. Then Moses heard the voice of God ordering him to escape with his people from the land of Egypt. This was a daunting task which made Moses hesitant, especially as Moses had a stammer which carried with it some insecurity, but God reassured him that he would provide for Moses and allow Moses' brother, Aaron to accompany him in this historic task. Moses then agreed.

But when Moses and Aaron confronted the Pharaoh with the demand of Israel's God to free his Hebrew slaves, the Pharaoh adamantly refused because he needed his Hebrew slaves for his many construction projects. The God of Israel, through Moses, unleashed the ten famous plagues to harass Egypt, or so Genesis suggests. These plagues included:

Blood in the Nile River
Frogs
Bugs
Wild animals
Pestilence
Boils
Hail
Locusts
Darkness
Death of first born

One could understand why these plagues could occur in Egypt of thousands of years ago. Sanitary conditions were primitive, bacterial disease was prevalent at a time when bacteria where unheard of, and infection, or pestilence, was an unknown word, as was the prevention of same, etcetera down the line of the list of ten. That they all occurred within a relatively short period of time would be incomprehensible today, but perhaps may not have been so thousands of years ago under such primitive conditions. Nevertheless, the effect on the Pharaoh was drastic enough that he told the Israelites to go.

After the Hebrews did leave, the Pharaoh changed his mind and ordered his army to apprehend them and force them to return to Egypt.

However, this attempt did not succeed because Moses and his followers, the Israelites, or Hebrews, were able to flee across a water obstacle that had miraculously parted for them, but then reassembled and drowned the attacking Egyptians.

The Hebrews, after a difficult journey led by Moses, now reached Mount Sinai where God gave him the Ten Commandments written on stone tablets. Since Moses took a long time returning to his people, they became restless and crafted a golden calf which they began to worship. When Moses finally returned and observed this heathen worship, he became furious and took God's stone tablets and used them to destroy the golden calf. He then crafted another set of stone tablets which had the Ten Commandments engraved on it. These tablets set the moral code that all of Moses Hebrew followers were to adhere to forever. These were:

1. *I am the Lord, your God, Who took you out of the land of Egypt, out of the house of bondage.*

2. *You shall not have the gods of others in My presence. You shall not make for yourself a graven image or any likeness which is in the heavens above, which is on the earth below, or which is in the water beneath the earth. You shall neither prostrate yourself before them nor worship them, for I, the Lord, your God, am a zealous God, Who visits the iniquity of the fathers upon the sons, upon the third and the fourth generation of those who hate Me, and [I] perform loving kindness to thousands [of generations], to those who love Me and to those who keep My commandments.*

3. *You shall not take the name of the Lord, your God, in vain, for the Lord will not hold blameless anyone who takes His name in vain.*

4. *Remember the Sabbath day to sanctify it. Six days may you work and perform all your labor, but the seventh day is a Sabbath to the Lord, your God; you shall perform no labor, neither you, your son, your daughter, your manservant, your maidservant, your beast, nor your stranger who is in your cities. For [in] six days the Lord made the heaven and the earth, the sea and all that is in them, and He rested on the seventh day. Therefore, the Lord blessed the Sabbath day and sanctified it.*

5. *Honor your father and your mother, in order that your days be lengthened on the land that the Lord, your God, is giving you.*

6. *You shall not murder.*
7. *You shall not commit adultery.*
8. You *shall not steal.*
9. *You shall not bear false witness against your neighbor.*
10. *You shall not covet your neighbor's house. You shall not covet your neighbor's wife, his manservant, his maidservant, his ox, his donkey, or whatever belongs to your neighbor.*

These guidelines for the Jewish religion, as well as other future beliefs, had taken form and would be the foundation around which religion was structured. From these Ten Commandments emanated religious, social, and moral edicts. These remain in the Torah, or Old Testament, to this day. Moses is given credit for forming and strengthening the drive to religion and the basis of Hebrew culture. He is also revered in other major religions.

God gave Moses instructions to form a shrine to be carried with the Hebrews until they reached their destination of Canaan, but when they arrived at Canaan's outskirts, Moses sent twelve scouts into Canaan who returned and reported that the country was populated by giants causing the Israelites to not enter the land. This angered Moses who told them that before they would enter Canaan, the current generation who was afraid of entering would have to die out necessitating that they would wander the wilderness forty more years.

Forty years later, Moses brought his followers to Canaan, passed on his authority to his brother, Joshua who led the Hebrews into Canaan. Moses never entered. He was not allowed to as a punishment from God because, as the story goes, when water was running short, God told Moses to "talk to the rocks." Instead, Moses struck them. For this transgression, God forbad Moses to enter the Promised Land He died, and was buried, but his burial site is unknown. It seems that God was a tough taskmaster, unforgiving of a minor infraction from a man who had done God's bidding for many years. However, it seems that in God's views about the religion he hoped humankind would develop, an infraction of any kind was major requiring some positive action.

Moses is revered as a prophet in four religions: Judaism, Christianity, Islam, and Baha'i. It is believed that Moses also authored the Torah (first five chapters of the Hebrew bible.)

The centuries were witnessing the slow and steady formation of the concept of religion. Their motives centered on an individual moral code as well as a world-wide moral code. History would prove they succeeded with some in the first goal, but the second, as yet, leaves much to be desired.

JOSHUA AND THE TIME OF JUDGES

Joshua played an active part when Moses led the Israelites out of Egypt through the torrid desert. He was one of the twelve spies that Moses sent into Canaan. Eventually, after Moses died, Joshua took over leadership and led them into their conquest of Canaan. Before Joshua died, he divided up the land amongst the twelve tribes, each self-regulating. **Judges 21:25** *In those days, there was no king in Israel, everyone did what was right in their eyes.*

The Time of Judges extended from 1244 BCE to 879 BCE. They were men and women steeped in military and spiritual matters, as well as having a deep knowledge of Torah. This "Judges" period of Jewish history lasted 365 years.

Who were these Judges? There were seventeen of them in this time period. Some of them had great influence on Jewish history, and their names will be familiar to all who are interested in the history of religion; a religion which Jews were trying to develop for the sake of mankind, but because of which, they faced hatred, derision, and death.

For instance, the first judge was Deborah. She made herself available to all by sitting under a palm tree where she dispensed advice of all kinds including battle instructions, necessary as they had to battle the Canaanites. One specific battle of the Jews was against a superior Canaanite force with 900 chariots against Israel's none. Things were looking bleak, but suddenly an unexpected rainstorm turned the ground into mud completely neutralizing the Canaanite force. Was the God of Israel responsible for this miracle?

Another famous judge was Samson, well known for his unbelievable strength. In his era, the Philistines, a seafaring tribe, were his enemy who, once they migrated to Israel's territory, were constantly at war with

Samson's tribe for control of the coastal areas. As you can see, warfare was still the norm amongst mankind at that time. The idea of religion, of course, was to negate that trend slowly but surely over time; a noble goal never to be reached, even as a number of religions finally evolved. Future history would demonstrate that lack of progress. If the goal was to saturate the world with religious premises as a way of creating a world-wide blissful peace—it still remains a work in progress.

Samson was born to a couple who, unable to conceive, was told by an Angel of the Lord that they would have a son who would deliver the Israelites from the Philistines. Samson who was dedicated to the God of Abraham had superhuman strength attributed to his long hair. His goal was to neutralize the aggressive Philistines, the enemy of Israelites. To better understand his sworn enemy, the Philistines, he takes a Philistine wife. She is killed by other Philistines, so Sampson turns his attention to another Philistine woman known as Delilah, to whom he comes very emotionally attached. Delilah takes advantage of Samson's attachment and is able to get him to reveal the secret of his strength—his long hair. Delilah cuts off his hair while Sampson sleeps. He is then easily captured by the Philistines who blind him and then place him in prison while he awaits a public execution in a temple of a Philistine God. Samson prays for revenge, places himself between two large pillars and shouts. **Judges: 28-30** *"Let my soul die with the Philistines!"* Sampson then pulls down the two pillars on himself and on the heads of all the Philistines.

SAMUEL—SAUL—DAVID

The Jewish period of the Judges lasted almost 400 years. During this time a central leadership did not exist as each judge was responsible for a single specific group of individuals. Samuel was the last judge. All the judges were required to promote a high level of individual responsibility. They also had to make certain that their followers were all on the same page as regards strictly keeping the religious laws that have been developed over time to guarantee appropriate ethical and moral behavior amongst themselves and their neighbors. If they did not, they believed God would alter their wayward course by causing their enemies (Canaanites, Philistines) to disrupt their activities by war—a difficult way to exist. A change was needed: Samuel was asked to anoint a king to rule the entire Jewish Community. **Samuel, 8:5-7** *And they the people said to Samuel "Behold, you have grown old and your sons do not walk in your ways. Now set up for us a king to judge us like all the nations." And the thing was displeasing in the eyes of Samuel.*

For Samuel this was a difficult task, but God convinces him to comply. Samuel appoints Saul to function as King and gives him two years of on-the-job training. As it turns out, eventually Saul loses favor with God because of continued disobedience. God wants another appointee, and Samuel chooses David.

As has been mentioned prior, the Philistines were the perpetual enemy of the Israelites for centuries. They throw down a challenge to Saul by offering that a Philistine giant of a man named Goliath will fight an Israeli in a single combat that will decide a coming battle as the two armies face each other in the Valley of Elah. For forty days and nights the Philistine giant, Goliath, steps forward, challenging the Hebrews to a single one-on-one battle to decide the outcome. At this time, David, a young man who was there bringing food to his warrior Hebrew brothers, volunteers to fight the giant, Goliath. David refuses armor offered by Saul, and steps forward armed only with a sling and five stones, while his opponent was armed with a javelin and was covered with body armor. The Philistine cursed David by his gods, but David replies: *"This day the LORD will deliver you into my hand, and I will strike you down; and I will give the dead bodies of the host of the Philistines this day to the birds of the air and to the wild beasts of the earth; that all the earth may know that there is a God in Israel, and that all this assembly may know that God saves not with sword and spear; for the battle is God's, and he will give you into our hand."*

David, with his sling and stone, hurls his weapon at Goliath, strikes him on the forehead, and the giant falls dead. The battle has been joined and won. The Philistines flee in panic. David becomes leader when Saul dies. He conquered the south of Israel and Jerusalem prompting the northern tribes to join him, thus enabling David to form a single country that would last for about five hundred years. Finally a leader of the fledgling Jewish religion would establish a national Jewish homeland infused with a religion and ethics.

Another of his many talents was as a psalmist. He wrote many psalms, one of which was at the dedication of the temple in Jerusalem:

> *I will praise you, LORD!*
> *You saved me from the grave*
> *and kept my enemies*
> *from celebrating my death.*
> *I prayed to you, LORD God,*
> *and you healed me,*
> *saving me from death*
> *and the grave.*
> *Your faithful people, LORD,*
> *will praise you with songs*
> *and honor your holy name.*
> *Your anger lasts a little while,*
> *but your kindness lasts*
> *for a lifetime.*
> *At night we may cry,*

but when morning comes
we will celebrate.
I was carefree and thought,
"I'll never be shaken!"
You, LORD, were my friend,
and you made me strong
as a mighty mountain.
But when you hid your face,
I was crushed.
I prayed to you, LORD,
and in my prayer I said,
"What good will it do you
if I am in the grave?
Once I have turned to dust,
how can I praise you
or tell how loyal you are?
Have pity, LORD! Help!"
You have turned my sorrow
into joyful dancing.
No longer am I sad
and wearing sackcloth.
I thank you from my heart,
and I will never stop
singing your praises,
my LORD and my God.

SOLOMON

Solomon, son of David, was next in line on the throne as king of the Jews. This story starts with a dream of Solomon's where he is visited by God. Solomon apparently impresses God when he tells the Lord that his intentions are honorable in that he pledges wise and compassionate rule geared to benefit his subjects. Impressed with these noble intentions, God promises Solomon his full support and a long life. However, these goodness and mercy protestations by Solomon were not matched by his life style. He soon fell into lascivious behavior as he slowly accumulated 700 wives and 300 concubines of numerous backgrounds. Surrounded by all these women, he fell into the worship of false gods and idols.

In spite of all these bad habits, Solomon is given credit for many accomplishments:

The State of Israel was organized into 12 districts with each district represented in Solomon's governmental structure one month at a time.

This fairly represented all and set up an honest and equal taxing structure for the nation.

He assured a peaceful co-existence with surrounding neighbors.

He is responsible for the construction of the first temple on Mount Moriah in Jerusalem, an architectural wonder built over a seven year period.

He built up his army.

Peace reigned supreme as he developed a flourishing trade relationship with his neighbors, all the while becoming extremely wealthy.

Intellectually, he is credited with writing many psalms, the Song of Solomon, and the book of Ecclesiastes as well as 1005 songs and 3000 proverbs.

Solomon is recognized as possessing God granted wisdom. One example of this is the famous episode where he settles a dispute between two women arguing over a newborn. It appears that they both gave birth to an infant at the same time and in the same house. There were no witnesses to the births. One infant died leaving both mothers to argue that the surviving child "belongs to me." They came to Solomon to solve their dilemma. Solomon told them that the child would be cut in half and split between the arguing mothers. One mother agreed, the other mother pleaded that Solomon not kill the baby and told him to give the baby to the other mother. Solomon now knew who the true mother was. This story has persisted through the ages.

In essence, King Solomon had a dual personality—one good, one not very good. Using his skills as a diplomat, his alliances and the treaties he made with neighbors prompted a peaceful environment for his subjects. However, his personal life did not follow these tenets; he took advantage of his position to promote for himself "the lap of luxury," accumulating non-Jewish wives, multiple concubines, worldly treasures of all kinds; all turning his mindset away from God-like pursuits. Much of this life-style rubbed off on his subjects, so both he and many of his citizens met with disfavor in the eyes of the Lord prompting a punishment which took the form of a division of the nation into north and south both of whom viewed each other as enemies and competitors.

After Solomon's death, Rehobohm, one of Solomon's sons, took over control of the south, and the north was taken over by Jeroboam, a former employee of Solomon. These two men would never get along, beset by enduring jealousies, non-cooperation, wicked life styles, and worship of idols which doomed, over time any hopes for Israel unity. It is interesting to note how tortuous and difficult it is to get rid of bad habits, promote good habits, and steer a course to goodness and compassion for all—as yet, even in this modern era, an unobtainable goal.

ISRAEL FALLS

The southern and northern kingdoms of Israel were both unstable from the standpoint of their leadership, but the northern kingdom lasted 134 years less than its southern counterpart because of anti-religious idolatry worship. In the south, many of the kings were righteous in that they believed and practiced goodness and mercy. The best example would be Hezekiah, 14th in the line since King David, who ruled Israel from 590 to 561 BCE. This occurred after Assyria conquered the northern kingdom of Israel in 740 BCE. Assyria was one of the powers of the ancient Middle East that occupied what is today an area encompassing northern Iraq and southeast Turkey. The Assyrians exiled the ten northern tribes of Israel into Assyria and marched south in an effort to capture Jerusalem. Hezekiah recognized this threat, so he began an ambitious defensive project to fortify Jerusalem by creating walls and improving the water supply.

In 547 BCE, the Assyrians, led by Sennacherib attack the Israelites, but the Assyrian army was decimated by a plague rendering the attack unsuccessful. Sennecherib's own children murder him after he returns home. This murderous act represents behavior of the times and reason enough for the "religious" pioneers to attempt to reverse the "normal" behavior patterns of the day; a daunting task.

After Hezekiah dies, his son, Manessah, succeeds his father on the throne. The bible describes Manessah's behavior: *(2 Kings 21:2-6)* "*He did what was evil in the eyes of the Lord ... He erected altars to Baal ... He passed his son through fire, practiced astrology and read omens, and performed necromancy and conjured spirits. He was profuse in doing what was evil in the eyes of the Lord, to anger Him.*" And if this was not enough, Manessah even has his own grandfather killed. If this was the lineage that was expected to foster religion to promote good behavior for the world…it would appear to be an uphill battle…so far. *(IIKings21:11-14)* *"Because Manasseh, King of Judah has committed these abominations…and he caused even Judah to sin with his idols…I will wipe out Jerusalem as one would wipe a plate thoroughly, and then turn it upside down."*

King Amon follows Manassah to the throne and continued his sinful philosophy. He is followed by Josiah, a lover of God, who institutes religious reforms that unfortunately die when Josiah dies, but not before Josiah, recognizing that the invasion threat from Assyria remains real, decided to hide the Ark of the Covenant with its Ten Commandments. Its whereabouts are unknown to this day.

The world does not change as some of the Jews attempt to foster this change. This is because they are up against a world still basically living under the tenet that "might makes right." With this truism in place, we see that the Assyrian empire is now decimated by a new power known as Babylon. No different than any of their predecessors, the Babylonians, in 434 BCE, invade Israel in an effort to stake out their claim to all of the former Assyrian empire. They succeed and remove the current Jewish king, Yehoiyachin, who they then take to Babylon along with 10,000 captives they consider to be the cream of the Jewish crop. Now in control of the Jews and their land, the Babylonians appoint a King (their puppet) named Zedekiah. But the "puppet" fools his masters when he organizes a rebellion against them. This immediately prompts the Babylonian king, Nebuchadnezzar, to attack Jerusalem. This siege lasts two years and is characterized by its cruelness as the Jews are starved into submitting. *(Lamentations 4:4-5,8-10)* *The tongue of the suckling infant cleaves to its palate for thirst; young children beg for bread, no one extends it to them. Those who once feasted extravagantly lie destitute in the streets; those who were brought up in scarlet clothing wallow in garbage … Their appearance has become blacker than soot, they are not recognized in the streets; their skin has shriveled on their bones, it became dry as wood … Hands of compassionate women have boiled their own children; they became their food when the daughter of my people was shattered.*

The Babylonians enter the city of Jerusalem, slaughter many people and destroy the Temple. The year is 422 BCE. They carry out the ultimate revenge when they exile all the Jews from the Holy land, thus severing the Jew's relationship with their God and eliminating them from the

Land of Israel. The Temple along with the Ark of the Covenant stored therein represented permanence for the Jewish people; no longer were they wandering homeless around the known world of the time. Now, with their presence in the State of Israel centered around the Ark in its permanent home on the Temple Mount, they felt that they and their religion had arrived—but it was to be short lived; the Babylonians would see to that.

TIME FOR REVIEW

The early evolution of the Jew as a concept to promote a harmonious world was frustrated from the start. As can be seen from previous writings, those pioneers who attempted to change the world by fostering a mindset based upon goodness and religious precepts met opposition from most of the world's population who were steeped in a "what's in it for me" concept. The two philosophies were and remain incompatible.

If we jump through the centuries to today, we see that nothing has changed. The Jewish people have faced vicious persecution throughout the ages. Anti-Semitism has been rampant for centuries, and if anything, it increases over time.

Semite is defined as a member of various ancient and modern peoples who have originated in the eastern Mediterranean area. It includes Hebrews, Arabs, Canaanites, Phoenicians. Most of us define it to mean the Jew, so anti-Semitism means Jewish hatred, and as thousands of years have demonstrated, it persists to this day. Ancient and modern examples abound: the Pharoah of Egypt ordered all Jewish babies (Moses amongst them) thrown into the Nile River; in ancient Babylon the Jews were murdered and their property and valuables stolen; in World War 2, in what would become one of history's greatest slaughters, 6,000,000 Jews were done away with by Nazi Germany and other countries. Thank God we do not see such excesses today, but the hatred of Jews has persisted amongst many to this date.

So now let us try and view what we know about world origins from the teleological standpoint that states that the final causes or design or purpose of life exists in nature as opposed to being molded by God. If we except this thesis, then we must agree that the Big Bang theory representing the origin of the Universe resulted when, from an infinitesimally tiny point, there emanated an explosion that sped away (perhaps initially faster than light) and formed the universe, upon which we live on one small planet of the billions that are out there in space. On this small planet, at an appropriate distance from the sun causing the correct environmental framework suitable to life—we are here in a few billion years. But if you prefer to speak in terms of God as the creator, then he gets all the credit with statements such as "God spoke the word and the Universe came into existence." We all have the right to accept one theory or the other.

If we accept the theory that God's spoken word was enough to bring the universe into existence, then we must also accept the word that the Garden of Eden was a reality and when Adam and Eve ate of the fruit of the forbidden tree indicating the susceptibility to sin, evil permeated Earth's population through the ages necessitating that God undo his mistakes by bringing on the great flood to destroy all human life on earth—except for righteous Noah and family.

After the flood, however, sin returned as the human race again began to ignore God's tenets. Perhaps God would now try a different approach, so he chose a single nation of people that he felt would understand the importance of what he was trying to accomplish. These were the Hebrews (Jews) and the land he would grant to them would be Palestine where several thousands of years from the beginning, Jews finally reside…again. Viewing this development from an historical perspective, how permanent would that be?

CYRUS THE GREAT

Geopolitical change characterized ancient civilizations, and it was not long that the Babylonian empire ceased to exist. Cyrus the Great became king of Persia and took the place of the Babylonians, becoming the dominant figure in the Middle East. With this power, and with an eye on Palestine, Cyrus informed the Jews that they could move back to their homeland. When they agreed, both the Jews and Cyrus were overjoyed because the Jews, by moving back, could reestablish their religious base, rebuild Palestine and rebuild the Temple, which they did in the year 516 BCE. The Persians also benefitted by their close friendship with the Jews who were under a form of Persian control directed by a High Priest named Zerubabbel. This system worked well as Palestine flourished under the new Persian developed governmental structure where Jews had much autonomy and were able to refine their written law including a rule forbidding Jews from marrying non-Jews. This one rule, at the time and well into the future, stabilized the Jewish religion for centuries. As I review modern times in the United States of America, and note how Judaism has evolved from orthodox alone to three divisions—orthodox Judaism, conservative Judaism, and reform Judaism, what impact will this have on Judaism in the next several hundred years? The idea of a Jew not marrying a non-Jew under these divisions may persist for the orthodox, but will the other two divisions maintain their Jewishness as they intermarry?

At about this time, or somewhat prior, a new religion surfaced, pioneered by Zarathustra who formed a religion known as Zoroastrianism. This new concept "told us like it was." The universe was "schizophrenic," that is it had a dual personality. One was a force for good and the other was a force for evil. Which of the two would dominate? All of us, good and

33

evil, would be involved in a continuous struggle. All humans regardless of religion, all Gods, all the world would be involved. How would it be decided—or would it ever be? So far, we are not yet close to a resolution. The different battles, the different kings, the different states, the different Gods have not yet resolved the dilemma. Would they ever?

ALEXANDER OF MACEDON

What or who would be the next influence on the evolving Jewish religion? Would it be positive or negative? So far history is replete with examples of both. The next actor on the burgeoning religious theme was Alexander the Great. He was just one more of those who had dreams of spreading his influence around the world, in this case, for the benefit of Greece. In 332 BCE he conquered Persia eliminating their ruinous control over the Jews.

First he had to take complete control of Greece by uniting the nation that had been divided by factions. He performed this task with ruthless efficiency, turning Greece into a single collaborative empire. History is unsure whether Alexander accomplished this goal by assassinating his principle enemy, Phillip, but however it happened, Alexander was now free to act. He created a strong united Greek army that would play a vital role in the Middle East and influence the Jewish movement in the direction of Greek collaboration. In a twelve year march, Alexander succeeded in capturing virtually the entire known world at that time. He is quoted as crying after completion of this task "because there is no more world to conquer."

When he conquered Egypt he came upon Jews living in Israel who had been subjects of the Persian Empire when it was in flower. The high priest of the Jewish Temple, fearful of the ramifications that might ensue as the Greeks took over, attempted to meet Alexander the Great. When Alexander witnessed this, he bowed before the high priest. As the story goes, this was witnessed by one of Alexander's generals who asked the reason for the bow. Alexander explained that he did not bow to the high priest, but rather bowed to the God who appointed the high priest to that role after Alexander had a dream where he saw the high priest wearing the apparel he had on. Alexander's interpretation allowed him to conquer

Jerusalem without conflict and fostered a good relationship between Jew and Greek. This allowed Alexander to peacefully incorporate the land of Israel into his world-wide empire and develop a grateful relationship between two different cultures of outstanding accomplishment. From the intellectual standpoint, the Jews and Greeks admired each other; a situation that would drastically change when Alexander sickened and died after he developed a fever that lasted for ten days, the cause of which remains unknown. Alexander was only 32 years of age when he was felled by this unknown malady.

After Alexander's death, the relationship between Jew and Greek changed. The Ptolemaic kingdom in Egypt, originated by Alexander the Great, took hold. This secured Greek influence on a willing Egyptian population.

The rest of the former Alexander the Great's empire was controlled by one of Alexander's generals named Seleucis. He took over the Eastern provinces representing what today is Afghanistan, Iran, Iraq, Lebanon, and Syria, with also parts of Turkey and other smaller parts of the middle east.

The land of Israel fell between these two dynasties geographically, but found itself under Seleucid control ruled by King Antiochus. The great majority of Jews were true to their Judaic beliefs, but some did embrace Greek culture. Those that did not embrace Greek culture precipitated a war in the Seleucid controlled section. It started when Antiochus issued a directive that ignited a torch: he ordered the Jews to abandon their religion and forbad its teachings and practice. This direct threat to the practice of Judaism was a far cry from the peaceful and collaborative ways of Alexander. In 175 BCE, Antiochus appointed a high priest for the Jews named Jason, a Jew who had been greatly influenced by Greek culture. This eventually ended up in a civil war between the religious Jews and those Jews who embraced Greek culture.

Chaos remained supreme throughout the empire. From this point forward we see an amazing part of history when the Jews very existence was threatened. This threat brought to the fore a family famous in Jewish history—the Macaabeans (meaning hammer) led by an elderly priest named Mattathias and his five sons. Mattathias was ordered by soldiers of Antiochus to make sacrifices to pagan Gods, but he refused. However another Jew, fearing great violence against the Jews, offered to make the sacrifice. Feelings were running high; sides were being drawn, and Mattathias killed this Jew along with the King's soldiers and fellow Jews he viewed as traitors. Then he fled into the wilderness along with his five sons and a small guerilla army to plan warfare against the latest of many enemies of the Jews—the Greeks.

Mattathias soon died. His son Judas took control, and, although greatly outnumbered, decisively defeated his enemy. This made Antiochus realize that this was a serious threat necessitating overwhelming force, but the sixty five thousand men and horses still could not prevail against the determined Jewish enemy of ten thousand.

The Maccabees now entered Jerusalem and resumed all Jewish practices. The Jewish holiday of Chanukah especially commemorates the resurrection of the temple as its signature event. While the temple was being refurbished and dedicated, a miracle occurred. A small flask of oil that was expected to burn for one day was ignited by a priest, and miracle of miracles—it lasted for eight days. That is why Jews, when they celebrate the Chanukah holiday, light eight candles, one each day.

The Greeks were decisively defeated. The Jews prevailed again allowing the principle of one God to permeate civilization. This was the principle contribution the Jews gave to humanity, a remarkable accomplishment from so few a people.

PART TWO

FROM ONE CE TO 2018 CE

CHRISTIANITY

The development of Christianity occurred during a time when Judaism was under assault from nations such as Greece and Rome who objected to Judaism's monotheistic thought. These two important nations could never accept the idea of the exclusivity of the Jews being chosen by God. The Jews were handcuffed, under penalty of death, by those nations whose goal was to achieve world control; they were not ready to let their ideas of how to attain this goal be usurped by the Jews trying to foster a religion and impose it upon others. To the nations, world control demanded warfare against zealots who tried to usurp the natural order of power by promoting thinking and reasoning and goodness and mercy; words that were foreign to individual nation's grandiose concepts.

What we were seeing was a conflict between a budding religion (Judaism) with its concepts of mercy and goodness as opposed to nation states who viewed the religion as being in competition with their goals.

Jews believed that God would finally impose a rule of one individual descended from the line of David. There were two Jewish groups who had their own bits of disagreement. The two were the Sadduces who followed only the five books of Moses (the Pentateuch). The second Hebrew group was the Pharisees who advocated more radical doctrines such as resurrection and angels. Into this mixture was born Jesus Christ, who became the central figure in Christianity, and whose life we will now discuss.

He was born in 6 BCE in Bethlehem. Future Christians would believe that Jesus was born through an immaculate conception as his mother Mary was said to be a virgin. He was believed to be descended from David. The only thing we know from his childhood is that once, on a trip to Jerusalem with his parents, he was found in the Temple discussing issues with the elders. He worked as a carpenter in his early adulthood. He started a ministry after being baptized by John the Baptist at age 30. Following this, it is said that Jesus fasted in the desert for 40 days and nights. It is also said that he resisted temptation from the Devil.

Jesus started his ministry and accumulated a number of disciples who followed him wherever he went in the Land of Israel. On one occasion, he went into the Temple, saw the moneylenders at work and drove them out declaring that "my father's House is not a house for merchants." Again, as mentioned before, did this mean that Jesus truly believed he was the son of God? In time, Jesus accumulated an adoring crowd who followed his travels listening to his entreaties for all to practice goodness, mercy, and humility.

His fame grew and it was not long before adoring crowds proclaimed him the Messiah, the son of David. The Pharisees, however, did not accept this depiction. Tensions reigned. According to the gospels, when Jesus asked his disciples to describe who he was, it was only Peter who promptly answered, "You are the Christ, the Son of the living God." Jesus announced that his fate was to be killed, but he would arise from the dead after three days.

Then this story of the transfiguration was told: Jesus went to a mountain with three of his disciples. His face is said to have shined like the sun, and his body glowed and he spoke with Elijah and Moses. Then a clear voice said, "This is my beloved son, with whom I am well pleased; listen to him." Christians believe this supports Jesus as being the Son of God.

Priests and Pharisees, recognizing the adoration of the crowds, felt that Jesus was a threat to their authority, and that he had to be neutralized. It would start with his arrest. One of Jesus's disciples, Judas, told the high priests that he would deliver Jesus to them. This betrayal would cause Judas, overcome by grief, to commit suicide. Jesus was arrested, stood trial, was found guilty and condemned to death on the cross for claiming to be the Son of God. He was crucified on the cross and died.

But the scriptures describe that three days later, Jesus miraculously appeared to numerous people, but then, after forty days, he is said to have descended into heaven. It would fall to others to continue his mission on earth. **Matthew 28:19-20** *"Go therefore and make disciples of all the nations, baptizing them in the name of the Father and the Son and the Holy Spirit,* *teaching them to observe all that I commanded you; and lo, I am with you always, even to the end of age,"*

This would be the start of another religion—just as Judaism started centuries ago. Many of the Jesus disciples remained in Jerusalem, but most spread out to encompass the world. In doing so, wherever they went, they were met with violence, similar to the experience of the early Jews. History is replete with the record of many assassinated Christian martyrs.

They would learn, as the Jews learned, that changing a world mind-set was, to say the least, a difficult and frightening undertaking. These evangelists had the dangerous job of trying to change the hedonistic and superstitious thinking that encompassed most of the world of the times; a dangerous task.

The Roman Empire of the time was home to people of multiple persuasions, but anything that disrupted the social order was viewed with suspicion, and the Romans kept close observation on such potential negative influences. Anything at all that had the potential to disrupt Roman rule would not be tolerated. It was crucial that social order must be maintained, so the Romans would never be shy about removing anything they conceived as a negative influence on their rule. One of their favorite methods of dealing with Christians they viewed as too provocative was to utilize them as actors in the coliseum where they would meet a horrible death by the hand of gladiators, lions, fire, crucifixions, etc. Emperor Nero was notorious in this regard. Other emperors of Rome even outdid Nero, especially an emperor named Decius (249 CE-251 CE) who introduced anti-Jewish and anti-Christian laws demanding that all Christian bishops offer sacrifices to him. Another emperor named Diocletian (284 CE-305 CE) blamed Christianity for ignoring Roman power. His punishment was severe: he burned Christian churches, bibles, scriptures and forbad Jesus worship. This did not hamper the Christian movement, however, and it continued to grow. A famous Christian martyr took a page out of the Jewish religion's book when he chose death rather than make any proclamation contrary to Christ's teaching.

The members of the first two major religions of the world fought hard for their beliefs to the extent that they were willing to give up their lives rather than betray their beliefs. The Christian religion's focus, that would and could not ever change, was Jesus Christ at the head. All its ideals were based only upon the thinking of Jesus. Any rejection of same was not possible, and as the religion matured, it continued its principle focus to retain Jesus's messages verbatim. Also, any majority rule needed acceptance from all the areas of the Roman Empire.

A major war erupted between two emperors of Rome, Constantine and Maxentius. Constantine won this battle (The battle of the Milvan Bridge) which gave him sole control of the Roman Empire. Legend has it that Constantine had a vision, sent to him by a Christian God, who promised victory if the sign of the Chi Rho, which was Greek for the first two letters of the name of Christ, would be painted on the soldier's shields. Outnumbered, they still won the battle. It is suggested that this prompted Constantine to convert to Christianity, which he did and then reversed the anti-Christian thinking of his predecessors, He thus opened up his subjects to free thinking about Christianity when he removed the legal restrictions which had been an impediment to acceptance. This was formalized in his Edict of Milan: *"When you see that this has been granted to Christians by us, your Worship will know that we have also conceded to other religions the right of open and free observance of their worship for the sake of the peace of our times, that each one may have the free opportunity to worship as he pleases; this regulation is made that we may not seem to detract from any dignity of any religion."*

At last! A government of a major country had finally seen the light. A country is a country with its necessary laws, and a religion was a religion with its necessary concepts built around God. The idea of them being competing influences was done away with by Constantine the great. They could and should coexist with mutual respect for each other. This was a great step forward at the time, but, as the world would see, well into the distant future, a major government would try to eliminate a world famous religion, the oldest one in history.

True to his word, Constantine put some Christians in political office and he became a Christian himself faithfully adhering to its tenets. The evolution of this acceptance continued, and by the fifth century CE, the Christian religion became the official religion of Rome. This was a first. Now Christian worship could be done in public, and its original Jewish character changed to one of its own.

RABBI YEHUDAH HANASI

A century after destruction of the Second Temple, the Babylonian Jewish community would be the most populous in the world and be noted as the focal point of Judaism and Torah study. This would remain for over one thousand years. Students of this era also recognized that the growth of Judaism had resulted in their migration to central and northern Europe and even India, and there were Jews in Egypt for centuries. Israel, of course, had been the principle center where Torah scholarship flourished.

It took a remarkable insightful Rabbi named Yehudah Hanasi to recognize that with so wide a dispersal of Jews in a world where communication over distances was primitive and not conducive to instant togetherness, Jews in these various corners of the world would not be able to discuss concepts with other Jews in distant lands, so the cohesiveness, so necessary for collaborative growth and a single Torah development and dispersal would suffer, thus endangering the concept of growth and unified development of an important and evolving religion. Rabbi Yehudah tackled this problem head on in order to make sure the oral Tradition would be developed and disseminated fully for all to understand and accept. This was critical so that the Jewish religion and its concepts would be understood by all Jews wherever they may be.

The Torah has two parts: Written Law and Oral Law, or Oral Torah. The Oral Law, or Oral Torah, was told to sons and students, by fathers and teachers. Remember, God told Moses that he would give him the Torah and the commandments." The written Torah is complete, so it is felt that "commandments" refers to the Oral Torah, or Law. That is why Rabbi Yehudah Hanasi wanted to be sure that all Jews all over the world had a single agreed upon Oral Law codified in writings known as the Mishnah. Once this was complete, other Jewish scholars, known as Amoraim, expanded upon and clarified the Oral Law.

THE GREAT REVOLT

The heading of this chapter has the word great in it. Do not confuse that to mean that the great revolt results were successful. It was not. Mistakes were made leading to catastrophe for the Jews. The fact that the Jews failed at their revolt against Rome in 66 CE, and they are still around is a testimony to their resiliency, a fact we already understand as a result of many examples since Adam and Eve, or at least as far back as 2000BCE.

The Jewish revolt against Rome was no surprise. As time went on, Roman rule grew more and more onerous. Rulers controlling captured territory in those days had a responsibility to collect taxes for the ruling empire. Needless to say, there was then and probably remains now an impetus to collect more than the conquering state required; the difference going into the pocket of the collector. Another onerous effect of being under foreign control was that the "controller" country appointed the high priest, which meant that the Jewish high priest remained beholden to the occupier.

Jewish protest would be expected to take the form of military resistance. It did indeed as a Jewish army known as the Zealots fought back. The assault on the Jews religious and political inroads demanded it; an attitude that most certainly played a part in Jewish survival throughout history.

Once the Roman Emperor, Caligula, came on the scene in 39 CE, things worsened. He declared himself a god and ordered that a statue of him be set up in the Temple. The Jews adamantly refused and prepared for a violent reaction from Caligula, but it never happened as Caligula was killed, apparently a victim of his own troops.

A Jewish revolt was always smoldering. It took form when Rome's contempt for Judaism became more obvious when the Romans defiled the Temple and favored the gentiles who also lived in Israel. These factors combined to precipitate warfare.

In the year 66, a Roman stole a large amount of silver from the Temple. This infuriated some Jews who then started killing Roman soldiers, which precipitated a Roman attack. The Jews effectively fought off a Roman garrison brought in from Syria, but the Jews could not prevail against a second Roman force of 60,000 who attacked the Galilee in Northern Israel. It is estimated that 100,000 Jews were killed or sold into slavery.

The Jews in Jerusalem felt that they could not win, so they did not support the northern Jews who were attacked. The embittered surviving Jews in the north fled to Jerusalem and killed Jews there who did not share their radicalism. Soon there were no Jews left standing. The amazing fact here is that all the Jews killed were killed by fellow Jews.

In 70 CE, the Romans entered Jerusalem. They participated in violence that ended with the destruction of the second temple. From this time forward there would be no formal Jewish presence in Israel for almost 2,000 years, or until 1948 CE, three years after World War II when the State of Israel was established.

In 132 CE, a new leader emerged on the Land of Israel scene. His name was Shimon bar Kokhba, and he led the Jews in a third war against the Romans. The hopes of the Jews were uplifted considering that bar Kokhba was descended from the Davidic Messianic dynasty. The revolt lasted three and a half years, but their hopes were violently dashed when the Jews were vanquished in a final battle at Bethar in the Judean Hills where every Jew was killed including bar Kokhba.

RABBI AKIVA

The death of Rabbi Akiva, is thought to be about the time of the Bar Kokhba event. He was not a warrior, as so many Jews had to be in order to counter the constant opposition thrown their way by numerous civilizations. He was instead a student of Judaism—with a fascinating story which I will try to relate at this time.

He sprung from mostly unknown and humble beginnings, but no one would even know of his existence until he was more than forty years of age. Akiva himself defined his early status as that of an am ha-aretz, meaning an illiterate. He learned to read and write and study Torah at age forty— and that itself is a fascinating and unusual story that deserves to be told.

Akiva's wife, Rachel, was the daughter of a man for whom Akiva worked as a shepherd. Her angry father, in response to her marriage, disowned and disinherited her. Needless to say, this left the freshly married couple in a bind to say the least. How would this couple cope with these circumstances? The story has it that Akiva's wife either encouraged him to study Torah, conceivably recognizing his innate brilliance, or demanded that he do so as a stipulation to continue the marriage. Akiva's Torah education took place, bringing to the fore a scholar of extensive brilliance. Perhaps, the lateness of his start and his maturity when he started combined to produce a recognized Torah scholar that will be remembered for time immemorial. **Deuteronomy 30:20** *"that you may love the Lord your God, that you may obey his voice, and that you may cling to Him, for He is your life and the length of your days: and that you dwell in the land that the Lord swore to your fathers, to Abraham, Isaac, and Jacob, to give them."*

After the bar Kokhba rebellion, Rabbi Akiva handled the decree by Rome that forbad the Israelis to study the Torah by convening public assemblies to teach Torah. A friend said to him, "Are you not afraid of

Rome?" Rabbi Akiva answered: "Let me tell you a story. Here is what I compare this to. Take a fox walking along the river. There are fish scattering in all directions. The fox said to them, "What is wrong?" They said to him, "We are trying to dodge the nets thrown in the water." The fox said to them, "Come up on the land and live with me. After all did not our ancestors live together years back?" The fish replied, "You are supposed to be clever, but you are not. If we are afraid in water, which gives us life, then in a habitat where we could die, we must not go."

After the destruction of the Second Temple (70 CE) when the Jews had lost their focal point, Rabbinic Judaism developed and the sages, like Akiva, became known as Rabbis. This changed Judaism so that Torah study became its center structure. Akiva continued his study with famous Rabbis and was ordained in 93 CE, and eventually started his own academy in Lod.

Akiva made the assertion that the Torah in its entirety, including the Ten Commandments, came from heaven. He also systematized the Mishnah (Jewish oral law).

Akiva would die a horrible death when he was accused of publicly teaching Torah, forbidden by the Romans. He stood before a Roman judge. In spite of this Akiva noted it was the time to recite the Shema prayer, so he did with a smile on his face. This practice was also forbidden by the Romans. Akiva was tortured to death—a martyr who would rather die than suppress his Judaic commandments.

Perhaps in this philosophy lies the secret of Jewish long term success over the centuries.

MUHAMMAD AND ISLAM

In 610 BCE, Muhammad was forty years of age and in Mecca when he started reciting what he perceived to be revelations from God. Others in his circle faithfully recorded these revelations into a document that would come to be known as the Quran. Muhammad's entreaties to his followers were not appreciated by the Mecca Saudi Arabian authorities. Feeling that he was usurping the social order of the community, they began to persecute Muhammad and his adherents. This persecution lasted 12 years, forcing Muhammad to immigrate to Medina, another city in Saudi Arabia, where he became successful in establishing his new religion and developed its constitution. In addition, he established rights for Jews, Christians, and pagans. These rights included:

Religious freedom
Security of the community
Security for women
Medina sacredness where no weapons were allowed
Violence prohibited
A fair tax system
Protection for all individuals regardless of religion
Rules for any political alliances
A legal system specific to each religion
A judicial system for each religion according to their beliefs

Now it would be time to sit back and assess the outcome. Within two years, two wars were fought over these issues: the first was the Battle of Badr which ended in a Muslim victory. This cemented the Islamic State propounded by Mohammad. A second battle, the Battle of Uhud 625 CE turned out to be inconclusive. In essence, Mohammad was able to stabilize the Islamic religion in place. By the time Mohammad died at age 62, the religion had successfully survived the usual birth-pangs. Many now converted to Islam, and in 632CE the Saudi Arabian tribes were united into the one religion of Islam.

Now, all of the three major religions had gone through very rough birth pangs.

From 632 CE to 750 CE much civil strife would batter the infant religion. New "Caliphs" arose to lead the religion, some of whom would be killed, but that did not hinder Islam's growth. The killings and internal conflicts did cause a schism to develop in the ranks necessitating a division in the religion; those that accepted the leadership of the first four leaders of the developing religion became known as Sunni Muslims, and those who only accepted a rule by one of the leaders, Husayn Ibn Ali, and his future descendants became known as Shia Muslims who were and remain in the minority. Ali was killed in one of the many battles that occurred in these formative years. Interestingly enough, religious minorities—Christians and Jews—often entered these Muslim wars in order to help the Muslims take over some of Byzantine and Persian lands. In these early formative years of religious evolution, many did not differentiate between the religion they were trying to organize and the nation states that had developed.

The next era of the Muslim religion from 750 CE to 1258 CE is considered the golden era in Muslim history; the Muslims spread their influence world-wide and they organized and built the first hospitals.in the history of the world. In addition, they are the first to formalize physician training and the licensing of physicians. They were actively involved in science advances, and Ibn al-Haytham is considered to be the pioneer in the development of the scientific method. In 859 CE, they organized the first university that ever awarded degrees. They pioneered these advances, and steadily grew to become the second largest religion in the world by population, second only to Christianity.

They enjoyed stability for centuries, but this stability became eroded in more modern times when some of the non-Muslim countries in the Muslim neighborhood usurped Muslim authority. These non-Muslim countries, having in mind their need for boundaries and protection, took control of Muslim lands as a means of cementing their self-protection needs. Never mind that this interfered and disrupted the religious foundation of those countries. Needless to say, the religious leaders were dismayed and saw these interventions as a continuation of the crusades that so decimated Muslim lands of old. Dedicated Islamists needed to use crusader language to remind all Arabs about the past Christian Crusades that had so decimated the Arab world. This changed the thinking of some in the direction of militancy, giving birth to Militant Islam. The marriage of religion and government was their ideology. Its purpose was to organize one unified powerful force that would structure the country around specific guidelines for individuals and strong political guidelines for the country. What is the history of this philosophy?

The first jolt occurred in 1798 CE when Napoleon of France invaded and defeated Egypt. This sent shock waves through the Arab Islamic world. How did they become so vulnerable? Where was their power base? There could be no Islamic future without a return to strict Islamic rules of governance and morality.

In Egypt, Gamal Abdel Nasser was elected president in 1956 CE. Hopefully a secular Arab- nationalism would evolve after overthrowing the now British rule of the country. It did not work. Nasser's failure to improve the economy, and his battle with dissenters and the failure of the Arabs in Israel's six day war turned Egyptian support in favor of the militant Islamists.

Hassan al-Banna, founder of the Muslim Brotherhood wrote, "Rebuilding the international prominence of the Islamic Umma by liberating its lands, reviving its glorious past, bringing closer the cultures of its regions and rallying around one word until once again the long awaited united and the lost Khilafah is returned."

It is clear that militant Islamists view the old crusades as an ongoing attempt by the West to subjugate and control Muslims. This philosophy would energize many Muslims around the world. The radical and angry Muslims embittered with their minds full of "crusader" mentality, became more and more radical to the extent that they recently hijacked four airplanes, flew them to iconic American destinations, and eagerly crashed into them, killing many Americans as well as themselves. All this while their leader, Osama Bin Laden, observed probably from the comfort of some cave. This is an example of the extent of the dedication and hatred for the "crusaders" that had evolved in the Muslim world—a hatred that has not abated for many years even after Bin Laden had been killed, and his place taken by a number of dedicated followers. Two great civilizations remain at war to this day.

The conflicts between religions and governments go back 2,000 years. Will it ever end?

Let us go back to the ongoing Jewish story where I left off.

ISLAMIC CONQUEST OF JERUSALEM

In the early days of religion, regardless of which one, the idea of war was omnipresent. Although the various religions established their individual religious principles, war as a political method for control, was never negated by any of the three major religions that had, by the 600's CE evolved in the world: these were, in order of their ascension, Judaism, Christianity, and Islam.

In 572 CE to 591 CE, a war was fought by the Persian Sassanian Empire and the Eastern Roman Empire known as the Byzantine Empire. In 614 CE, Jerusalem fell to the Persians who apparently looted the city and killed its 90,000 Christian inhabitants. War was war in those days; enemies were to be killed, as was property to be destroyed as manifested by the looting of the Christian Church of the Holy Sepulchre where they captured the true cross which they initially kept, as it was a Christian holy relic. The one bit of good news in all this is that the cross was returned to Jerusalem in 628 CE by the victor. I suppose this to be a bit of generosity showing how good the victor can be after the wanton destruction and murder. It is said that the Jews participated in the war against the Persians. It must be difficult to give up old habits—but again these "old habits" were apparently considered the norm in those days.

Muhammad died in 632 CE. Who would succeed him? Let's solve it the old fashioned way—have a few wars. Once the wars were over, a Caliph, a spiritual leader of Islam, who claims succession from Muhammad, named Abu Bakr took control. What do new Caliphs do? Start more wars of course, but now we will learn a very novel way that Muslims do this. Here are the steps:

Differentiate among the tribes to determine which ones you want to conquer for the benefit of Islam's growth and spread.

Once identified, call the Azaan. This is a beautiful song, sung by a man with a beautiful voice that could be heard by the tribe identified. This song basically sends a message: talk to us, or be destroyed by us. If the identified tribe sings back it means they have chosen conversation, whereupon the tribe will hear the full terms necessary to stay alive; terms such as taxes, tribute, obedience etc. Failure to accept full submission will result in the sword.

Those who do not sing back have sent a message that they choose war, for which they will usually, but not always, not have a long wait. To the victor, belongs the spoils.

In 634 CE, Abu Bakr died and was succeeded by Umar who continued warring, but did suffer a defeat at the battle of Yarmouk; Muslims against Christians. The Muslims then made a decision to attack Jerusalem. They decided upon a bloodless siege by encircling the city. This had a positive effect as the Muslims prevailed after four months; Jerusalem surrendered. In essence, the Jews in the area were saved by the Muslims from the Christians.

More than one-half century after the capture of Jerusalem, the Muslims built the Dome of the Rock, which signified and solidified Muslim rule over the Middle east for 400 years, or until the next change (more later).

EIGHTH CENTURY JUDAISM

Gaonim in Hebrew refers to 'the magnificent'. We introduced them briefly before. They were the final authorities on Halachic law; an interpretation of the laws of Jewish scriptures. This period lasted 450 years during which time these geniuses, 80 of them, labored on this difficult task while remaining anonymous except for their names. The Goanim wrote the first Jewish prayer book and also wrote books on Jewish belief in language understandable by all. These writings have become "the gospel," so to speak, which have become unimpeachable standards.

Principally, Jews lived in two locations during this period. The first location, under Christianity, was in Asia Minor. The second location was in the area where Muslim Arabs resided. Jews were better off in the Muslim regions of the Middle East where they were viewed with a greater amount of tolerance. Jews had already spread throughout the Roman Empire long before the fourth century when its rulers became Christian. After the fourth century, this religious change of the rulers was detrimental to the Jews as the Christians viewed the Jews as "Christ killers", or in more gentle terms as a "nefarious sect". It is mostly in Palestine where this mind-set persisted. Jews in other parts of the Roman Empire were more readily accepted. In Palestine during the days of Jesus, it was reported that some of the Jews clamored for his death by crying out to Pontius Pilot, the Roman leader, "His blood be upon us and our children". It would take until 1965 CE when the Vatican, under Pope Paul VI, declared that that the Jewish people cannot be collectively held responsible for the death of Jesus.

In the early seventh century in Spain, Jews had to undergo forced conversions, but later in that century it had all changed. Spain, under the Muslims, became the area where Jews became fully integrated. In addition, Germany became another center where Jews flourished. But the hostile nature of Jewish history pushed Jews into separate enclaves where they became easy targets, especially as they have developed economic influence in competition with their non-Jewish neighbors. Mostly, the only economic influence open to the Jew is that of a money lender, a profession not geared to make friends. In tough economic times, this is the first occupation that may not survive and soon the aggrieved take it out on all Jews. In Germany in 1096 CE angry crowds assembled to participate in crusades against Muslims ostensibly to punish them for taking Christ's sepulchre in Jerusalem. And if we are going to do that to the Muslims, let's warm up with the Jews who did worse—they killed Jesus Christ.

The crusaders, on their way to the Middle East, decide on this last course; they attack Jews in six major German cities and kill them all. Then they invaded Prague in Czechoslovakia and killed all the Jews there. On their way through Hungary, the Hungarian king tried to reason with the crusaders in terms of allowing peaceful pass through the country, but things get out of hand necessitating that the King called in the army. In the ensuing conflict, all the crusaders were killed. Many Jews and Christians die.

A new slander evolves in the 12th century CE. The Jews commit ritual murder of Christian children. This blood libel, leveled at the Jews, is an excellent example of what the Jews have had to deal with over the centuries. In 1104 CE England, authorities found a dead body in a forest. He was a young man found hung to death—and the rumor started that he was killed by Jews in order to have blood so as to make Matzos for the Passover holiday. It would take a while, but this libelous assertion would be repeated as an explanation for deaths many times in the future, and in numerous countries until it became dogma. Example: in the year 2014 CE, a Hamas spokesman was quoted on a Lebanese television interview: "We all remember how the Jews used to slaughter Christians in order to mix their blood in their holy matzos. This is not a figment of imagination or something taken from a film. It is a fact acknowledged by their own books and by historical evidence." He had no evidence in substantiation. This falsehood adds to the Jewish woes as they face more threats against them.

Then their position as moneylenders to the wealthy suffers in the 13th century when a banking system develops. In all countries, the necessity of Jews as moneylenders has now come to an end, and they are expelled from both Britain and France.

In 1348 CE and 1349 CE the Bubonic Plague decimates Europe. This is a fatal bacterial disease which causes massive lymph node swelling and fever which leads to death. At that time, however, bacteria were unknown and superstition prevailed. Who better to blame for this catastrophe than the Jews even though they died from the Plague like the many others; and the word went out that "The Jews poisoned the wells." They were burned to death by the tens of thousands. The survivors fled in the direction of Poland. Fortunately, the King of Poland had a Jewish girl friend so he welcomed Jews into his country.

And since my great grandparents were from Poland before they immigrated to the United States, I have to wonder if perhaps some of my ancestors were part of this exodus.

RASHI—RABBI SHLOMO YITZCHAKI

Rashi was born in the year 4800 CE. He was born in France to a father considered to be a great scholar. From age 17 to 25, Rashi embarked on a serious study of Torah study with the great scholars of his time. Following this, he studied more on his own. Rashi became a Rabbi in the town of his birth and continued to study until he felt confident in his written analysis. He had an unusual way of testing whether his Torah commentaries were worthwhile. He wrote each analysis on parchment, did not sign them, and visited many Torah academies were he would leave his parchment analysis. He never disclosed who he was. I believe this was a clever way to get his message across; and making it incognito gave the reader the inability to be swayed in any way by knowledge of the author. Those who read Rashi's analysis, and were so impressed by the brilliant interpretations, could only assume that they must have been written by God himself. Rashi continued his subterfuge with many Torah academies. One time, he was caught inserting one of his parchment interpretations in the usual location. The cat was out of the bag. The author was identified. Rashi's name became instantly famous and he became the ultimate authority on Torah scholarship. To study Torah today without Rashi's commentaries as the final authority would be unthinkable.

He died at age 65. He had no sons, but he did have two daughters who had sons, and his grandchildren and sons-in-law followed in Rashi's footsteps.

MAIMONIDES

Speaking of geniuses, this gentleman leads the pack. He is considered probably the most intellectual Jew of all time. He was a Jewish scholar, philosopher, physician, legal authority, political consultant. He served the Jewish and multiple other communities. His real name was Moshe ben Maimon, "Moses, son of Maimon" also known as Rambam. He was born in Spain in 1137 or 8 CE and was raised in the city of Cordoba. His father taught him Jewish subjects.

When Rashie was ten years of age, a Muslim sect known as the Almohad dynasty took over the country and reversed the peaceful philosophy of co-existence with all religions that Maimonides and his family lived under. His Jewish family, as well as all other Jews and Christians were given an offer they could not refuse. When Maimonides was ten years old, the Almohad Dynasty, a strict sect of Islam, took over and presented all Jews with three choices: conversion, exile or death. Of course they chose exile and the family left for Morocco. It is thought that Maimonides was about twenty years of age when they emigrated. He outwardly practiced Islam, apparently for protective purposes, but practiced Judaism in secret. In 1165 CE, the family visited Israel which was under Crusader rule, and finally settled in Egypt.

He worked as a physician full time, but in spite of this he managed to write the Mishneh Torah and the Guide to the Perplexed, both documents describing Jewish life. The Mishneh Torah took fourteen years to complete. It consists of fourteen books with 1000 chapters. The guide to the perplexed was written so that students of Torah would have a groundwork foundation to understand that there was no incompatibility between scripture and reason. Maimonides died in 1204 CE.

INQUISITIONS

Religious institutions were still strict by the fourth century CE. The Catholic Church developed tribunals whose purpose it was to evaluate anyone suspected of heresy, defined in the case of the Catholic Church or any church for that matter, as a belief that does not agree with the Church's official tenets. After all, if anyone professes membership in a particular church it should be assumed that they agree with its rules. Those who do not or those who are hiding the fact that they do not, are committing heresy. Since that had the potential to be very disruptive to the effective functioning of a church, its leaders agreed it must be stopped. The penalty for Christian heresy was usually excommunication from the church, but in its early years with the church and state being so intimately connected, the penalties were severe punishment up to and including death.

These inquisitions took place in four different time periods.

Medieval inquisition started in 1184 CE it includes the Episcopal inquisition (1184 CE-1230 CE) and the Papal inquisition (1230 CE). These inquisitions were the Catholic Church's reaction to popular movements that took place in Europe and were considered to be heretical. After 1230 CE, Pope Gregory IX changed direction in that he moved the authority for evaluation and punishment from the Bishops to the Papacy. The Pope would then assign two inquisitors to oversee the trial and conflict punishments. Their punishments varied depending on the judge and went as far as the heretic being burned at the stake.

Spanish Inquisition was established by King Ferdinand and Queen Isabella of Spain in 1478 CE, and approved by the current Pope at the time, who set up a royal system under the King and Queen managed by secular clergy who concentrated mostly on those Jews who agreed to be converted to Roman Catholicism, but were accused of never giving up Jewish rituals and practice. This royal inquisition also persecuted Protestants. The Spanish Inquisition's records of torture and executions of these Protestants who abandoned Catholicism is famous for its penalties. They tried 341,021 people, and executed ten percent.

The Portuguese Inquisition was established by the Portugal king operated similar to the Spanish Inquisition. It spread throughout the Portuguese Empire in India and Asia. Those penalized were converts to Catholicism who were accused of holding on to Hindu beliefs.

The Roman inquisition, started by Pope Paul III, was set up in 1542 CE, with the Pope establishing the Holy Office as the final arbiter for all heresy trials. It was staffed by cardinals as the final arbiters. This was the body that condemned Galileo for heresy for teaching that the earth and all the planets revolved around the sun. This organization persists to this day, being renamed as the Congregation of the Faith.

MARTIN LUTHER-- PROTESTANTISM

Martin Luther was a Roman Catholic who raised questions about Catholicism. For instance: he was disturbed by the fact that Popes could extract financial donations from the people to cancel out penance for sins that they had committed. This was only one of 95 examples developed by Martin Luther, which he posted on the chapel door of the University of Wittenberg. These examples were printed and disseminated widely throughout Germany and Europe. It set off a firestorm as Martin Luther was questioning some of the basic tenets of Roman Catholicism. They ordered Martin Luther to recant. This he would not do "unless scripture proved me wrong."

As a young man, his father hoped for a legal career for his son. Martin Luther started on this route in school, but an unusual experience caused him to change course and become a monk: once, caught in a severe thunderstorm, Martin Luther's fear for his life caused him to pray to St. Anne, "Save me, St. Anne, and I'll become a monk." True to his word, he went to a monastery. Afterward, he became a delegate to a conference given by the Catholic Church; was appalled by what he felt was their corruptive practices and became very upset. He earned a doctorate in theology at the University of Wittenberg and became a professor. He had a moment of truth when he realized that it was not important to fear God, but rather to believe that salvation will come via faith alone. When Martin Luther stated that the bible did not give exclusivity to the Pope in interpreting scripture, the Pope had had enough—on 1521 CE, he excommunicated Martin Luther from the Roman Catholic Church. In addition he was declared to be a convicted heretic and had to go onto hiding. He founded the Lutheran Church which became very successful over time. He married and had six children, became very ill and died at age 62 in 1546 CE.

His antithesis against Jews was legendary. Initially, Luther urged the Catholic Church to attempt to assimilate them. He urged the Church to treat the Jews fairly and make every effort to convert them. When he was told of Jewish efforts to convert Catholics, his thoughts turned 180 degrees and his next entreaties were as follows:

Jewish houses should be razed and destroyed.
Jewish writings should be taken from them
Rabbis should be forbidden to teach on pain of loss of life and limb
Self-conduct on highways be abolished for the Jew
Rabbis should be forbidden to teach under pain of loss of life and limb
Set fire to their synagogues and schools
All cash and treasure of gold and silver be taken from them

Jews could have a flail, an ax, a hoe, a spade put into their hands so young strong Jews and Jewesses could earn their bread by the sweat of their brow

There are those who believe that Luther, a German, paved the way to Adolph Hitler. This seems far-fetched, but one has to wonder what effect Luther's anti-Jewish entreaties could have had on some of the German population.

BLOOD LIBEL

This serious libel against the Jews has been mentioned before in this book. It is an excellent example of the irrational roots of anti-Semitism. Any evolved concept that could possibly result in the death of millions, as occurred in Nazi Germany in the early 1940's, deserves to be studied in as much detail as possible. It is a lesson that needs to be learned so as to avoid a similar potential for it, or anything like it, to be expressed in the future. Lives could still be at stake. We need to study the effects of anti-Semitism to be alert to any form of hatred that carries with it the potential to get out of hand and result in irrational violence against any religion, or any form of thought processes developed by human beings. The blood libel is a specific case in point. Its history deserves an intense scrutiny—so that it, or anything like it, never surfaces again.

Since I have mentioned in this book the possibility that Judaism may have started with Adam and Eve as has been proposed by some, or at least started with Abraham and Sarah, its roots obviously go way back. Through its early evolution there was no specific concept of anti-Semitism although all the religious pioneers had their initial prejudices levied against them. The first real signs of anti-Semitism began surfacing in the eleventh century after relatively good relations between Christians and Jews who had frequent contact, extending even to intermarriage. However, when the Christians, after the year 1000 CE began their own efforts at reorganization, there began a slow change in the thinking about Jews in a negative direction. This resulted in an evolution toward anti-Semitic thought which rubbed off on the Crusaders, so that the first crusaders initiated serious anti-Semitism in the Holy Roman Empire including in cities in what is now France and Germany. This serious anti-Semitism resulted in violence including massacres of Jews which heated up anti-Semitism to the extent that unfounded, violent, and vicious rumors began to spread about Jews. In 1144 CE, the straw that broke the camel's back resulted from the death of an English boy, William of Norwich, who was found dead with diffuse wounds over his body, arms, and head. A priest, who was a relative of the dead youngster, blamed the Jews, and from this unproven accusation there grew the theory that Jews crucified a Christian child in order to use his blood in their unleavened bread, necessary to celebrate the Jewish holiday of Passover. This became known as the blood libel, and it persists to this day. In more modern times in Damascus, Syria (1840 CE) and in Hungary (1882 CE), false confessions emanated from torture, but the accused were eventually acquitted. In 1911 CE, a man named Mendel Beilis was accused of ritual murder and was imprisoned for two years before an all Christian jury acquitted him. In the 1930's CE, the Nazis utilized the blood libel as part of their anti-Semitic propaganda. It has not yet died as it still surfaces in parts of Europe and the Arab world.

POLAND AND THE JEWS

This is the story of Jews in Poland. The country became Christian in the 1000's CE. It became part of Europe at the time and slowly and surely became a prominent nation-state. At this time, in order to advance their potential as a nation, they brought in consultants to assist in this complicated process. These consultants were Jews with experience in economics, accounting, banking etc., and their purpose was to help develop the nation economically. Understanding the prejudices of the time coupled with the knowledge of Jewish expertise and anti-Jewish prejudice, they were careful to document exactly what was expected of these 'consultants' so they formulated a charter which spelled out in intimate detail the rights and privileges and protections for these consultants. These were as follows:

If there is a question involving Jewish money or property, there must be testimony on the issue from both a Jew and a Christian. If a Christian causes any injury to the Jew, the accused is required to pay a fine. This had the effect of making sure that witnesses spoke nothing but the truth.

If the Christian causes damage to a Jewish cemetery, punishment is mandatory according to the law.

A Christian attack on a Jew will demand his punishment. The accusation of the blood libel is absolutely forbidden.

A Christian physical attack on a Jew must be identified promptly. If Christian neighbors fail to respond, they will be fined.

No one must accuse Jews of using the blood of human beings.

Jews are entitled to the same rights and privileges of Christians. They can buy and sell any legal goods, and if hindered in this process, the hinderer shall pay a fine.

One can clearly see that this interesting document had the benefit of the Jews in mind. Certainly, any Jew contemplating a position such as required by the Polish King needed this kind of protection before taking any position in a predominantly Christian land. Jews were slow to arrive in Poland initially, but when other countries started to expel its Jews, Poland, with these protections in place, became a magnet for the arrival of these Jews.

When Poland and Lithuania unified in 1569 CE, its borders were increased, opening up new opportunities for more Jews to become involved in managing the expanded country. The employed Jews were also given the right to organize and staff a yeshiva, an institute for Jewish learning. Jewish population of Poland increased from 1500 CE (50,000) to 1650 CE, (500,000). Jews of the time had found an excellent home with their own governing body. The Poles of the time did not interfere in any way with Jewish life. Commerce and scholarship flourished and expanded.

So far in this narrative, the reader would be inclined to believe that all was sweetness and light with the Jews of Poland. No exactly. They had their pressures. First of all, the Jews were required to work alongside Poles and Ukranians who still had a mindset of Jews as Christ killers. Needless to say tensions emanated from this at times. On one occasion, some Jews were accused of the theft of church property. They were tortured and burned at the stake. This of course was not legal in the new Poland. Never-the-less it occurred.

In 1635 CE there was extreme violence in Ukraine leveled against Jews and Poles that was neutralized by the authorities. However, 13 years later, a Ukrainian Cossack named Bogdan Chmielnicki started round two mostly aimed at Jews, 100,000 of whom were murdered via unbelievable torture, virtually too graphic to put into writing. They also completely destroyed 300 Jewish villages. Chmielnicki's anti-Semitism would only be matched by Adolph Hitler in the Second World War 1939 CE-1945 CE. To the best of my knowledge, there is still a statue of Chmielnicki in Kiev, Ukraine.

JEWS ARRIVE IN AMERICA

There are several classes of Jews who came to America as it was slowly being populated after Columbus's discovery. These classes are as follows: Sephardim who are descendants from Spain or Portugal and came in 1654 CE mostly from Brazil. They populated a number of Eastern Coast cities. The next group was Ashkenazi who came from Eastern Europe and Germany. The Sephardics remained dominant during the early days of the American Revolution, and the early synagogues adhered to Sephardic rituals.

Most Jews immigrated to the United States for one of two reasons: opportunities for entrepreneurship and the flight from anti-Semitism. In 1790 CE there were, at the most, 2000 Jews in America. The population slowly increased over the years so that by 1880 CE, 250,000 Jews, mostly Ashkenazi, had arrived. The effects of major pogroms in Eastern Europe resulted in a large Jewish exodus increasing the American population to 2,000,000 by 1914 CE when World War 1 started. These Jews mostly arrived from Eastern Europe principally from the Pale of Settlement including Poland, Russia, Belarus, Lithuania, Ukraine. By 1920 CE, the percentage of all Jewish immigrants had risen from five percent to 50 percent. This prompted immigration restrictions which remained in place through World War 2. Jews assimilated well in their new country. During World War 2, 550,000 Jews joined the U.S. military. Following the war, Jews had a tendency to move to the suburbs and fully integrated into American society both in community and school which resulted in increased intermarriage rates up to fifty percent. Also, after the war, the Jews joined the increasing migration to suburbia.

After World War 2 and the Holocaust, where most of the Jews in the European Jewish community were killed, the United States became the largest diaspora population in the world, so that by the early 2000 CE there were 5.3 million Jews in America.

There are three Jewish denominations: Orthodox, Conservative, and Reform. Orthodox Jews make up ten percent of all Jews. Their rules are strict, but they now are more modernized in that they interact fully with the surrounding secular society. Their principles include: the worship of one God, circumcision at eight days of life, haircut at age three and the wearing of a Kippah (head covering) for the first time, Bat mitzvah at age 12 for girls, and Bar Mitzvah at age 13 for boys. Both read from the Torah and commit to a Jewish life and vow strict adherence to Jewish holidays. Shabbat, from Friday evening to Saturday evening is a day of rest with very strict limitation of activities reminding orthodox Jews that God rested on the seventh day of creation. The other Jewish sects have similar Jewish rituals, but laxness in their completion is not uncommon.

Reform Judaism emphasizes the fact that the ethical aspects of Judaism are more important than the ceremonial aspects. In other words, there is less emphasis on ceremony and more on the ethical aspects. How did Reform Judaism develop? It arose in the early 1800s CE in Germany with the idea that Judaism should be given a modern push along the lines of western thought, but not in any way conflicting with Jewish principles. Was this possible? The orthodox Jew thought no, but the reform pioneers plowed ahead. They felt strongly that Reform Judaism's principles could be established that would not run afoul of orthodox principles. And as the structure of life and society had so changed, the Reform pioneers felt that it was a necessity to change, so they concentrated on Synagogue service changes and other areas involving Jewish activities that would not conflict with Orthodox objections. Moses Mendelssohn was the leading rabbi in this effort. The first Reform congregation was established in Hamburg in 1818 CE. Temple was the word used to replace the word Synagogue. The German language was introduced to the service, and an organ, similar to Christian services, was also introduced to accompany prayers. The Reform movement spread to other European countries including Austria, Hungary, Denmark, and Holland. In England it became established under the name of Liberal Judaism.

America was not to be left out, and started their brand of Reform Judaism under the direction of Isaac Mayer Wise who managed to establish the Hebrew Union College where the fist Reform rabbis were ordained. At their first graduation of rabbis, shellfish was served, a food absolutely forbidden by Jewish law. This caused consternation amongst traditional Rabbis and religious Jews. The back lash led to another Theological Seminary for the training of Conservative Rabbis, sort of a middle ground between Orthodox and Reform.

The Jews who came to America made impressive advances in all areas of American life.

THE PALE OF SETTLEMENT

Since the days of Abraham and Sarah who have the majority vote as to who were the founders of the first religion in the world, Judaism, the Jews have populated the earth—so to speak. They never came close to the volume of adherents such as evolved in Christianity and Islam, but their resilience, against all odds, has been staggering. As mentioned prior, they have a great majority population volume in Israel and have a substantial volume in the United States with lesser presence in many other countries. Against all odds, they are still here, the oldest religion in the world.

Pale is a word from the Latin (palus) meaning stake. A Pale refers to a specific section of a country defined by its own boundaries and governed by its own administration where a defined population has been ordered to settle. In the case of Russia, they had a well-known Pale of Settlement which was developed after Poland underwent three partitions in the late 1700s CE. Jews were not welcome in any other areas of Russia. It took until 1860 when some exceptions were made to this rigid geography of the Pale (where my grandparents lived) including all of Russian Poland, Lithuania, Belarussia—as Belarus was known at the time—much of Ukraine, Bessarabia, and the Crimean Peninsula. Jewish commercial rights were restricted to these areas for all except those highly educated Jews, medical professionals, those who completed military service, merchants and artisans.

Much of these loosening of restrictions were discontinued in the 1889s CE with the ascension of Tsar Alexander who developed "Temporary Laws" which forbad any other Jews to be allowed out of the Pale. Five million Jews lived therein, but it would change during World War 1 when very great numbers of Pale residents had to flee from the invading Germans prompting the Russian government to abolish the Pale concept on 1 April of 1917 CE.

As a reflection of the fact that nation states were suspicious of religion throughout past history, other nations had their own "Pales" where Jews, forced to live, were easier to observe and control. There were Pales in England, France and Ireland in 1171-2 CE. Northern France had its Pale from 1247-1558 CE. There are no Pales of Settlement as I write this book. We have outgrown them, thank God.

ALIYAHS

In Hebrew, making Aliyah has a double meaning: First It means being called up to read the Torah in the synagogue during religious services. This is an honor given to individual parishioners and those 12 year old girls who are called up to read a portion of the Torah during Bat Mitzvah services, or 13 year old boys being called up to do the same in their Bar Mitzvah. The second meaning of Aliyah refers to a "going up" to the land of Israel—the most important location for Jews where they make Aliyah and "go up" to pray. The land of Israel is central to Jewish history where Jewish Matriarchs and Patriarchs lived, and where two Holy Temples were built and destroyed; and where, hopefully, a third temple will someday arise. This is the thought that has persisted through many years in the Jewish psyche. Needless to say, resistance to this possibility has never abated throughout the centuries.

(Isaiah 11:12) *"He will raise a banner for the nations and gather the exiles of Israel; He will assemble the scattered people of Judah from the four corners of the earth."*

(Isaiah 43:5-6) *"Do not be afraid, for I am with you; I will bring your children from the east and gather you from the west. I will say to the north 'Give them up!' and to the south, 'Do not hold them back.' Bring my sons from afar and my daughters from the ends of the earth."*

(Isaiah 16:14-15) *"However, the days are coming," declares the Lord, "when men will no longer say, 'As surely as the Lord lives, who brought the Israelites up out of Egypt,' but they will say 'As surely as the Lord lives who brought the Israelites up out of the land of the north and out of all the countries where he had banished them.' For I will restore them to the land I gave their forefathers."*

The world patiently waited.

Throughout many centuries, there has always been some presence of Jews in the Land of Israel. They were there working to beautify the land, make it agriculturally viable, founded small towns and settlements, and revived the Hebrew language.

The first major Aliyah took place between 1882 and 1903. Its impetus was pogroms in Russia and resulted in 35,000 Jewish immigrants arriving in Israel. This was small compared to the several million who immigrated to the United States from the Russian Pale of Settlements as I have already related with my grandparents who arrived in the United States in 1904. Not surprisingly, these pioneers were beset by many difficulties such as disease, unfamiliar weather, very heavy Turkish taxation, and at times, fierce Arab opposition. It was only due to Baron Edmund de Rothschild's generosity that these settlements did not completely vanish. In spite of this, half of the settlers were forced to leave within a few years of their arrival.

The second Aliyah, again engendered in Russia by more pogroms, encouraged 40,000 younger citizens to immigrate to Israel. Half of them would eventually leave due to economic difficulties, but this Aliyah accomplished much when the pioneers managed to stabilize economic conditions, established the first kibbutz, laid the foundation for Tel Aviv, the first major city, published a Hebrew newspaper and founded political parties, in essence laying a foundation for a future state. World War1 interrupted further migration.

The next (3rd) Aliyah occurred from 1919 to 1924 and was engendered by more Pogroms plus the British conquest of the Palestine area and the Balfour Declaration, which was a letter, written from Foreign Secretary Arthur James Balfour of Britain to Baron Lionel Rothschild, expressing the governments support for a Jewish homeland in Palestine. World War 1, at the time, was not going well for the British and the Allies; although the presence of America, soon to join the struggle, was expected soon.

In the late nineteenth century, a national movement of the Jews developed known as Zionism. Its purpose was to establish a Jewish homeland in the area previously known as Canaan and currently known as the Land of Israel. In spite of much opposition from Arab countries, the Land of Israel came to fruition in 1948. Threats to its existence continue to this day.

The third Aliyah took place from 1919 to 1923 and was a continuation of the second.

The fourth Aliyah took place from 1924 to 1929, the result of increased Polish anti-Semitism and stiffened American immigration policies.

The fifth Aliyah occurred after the Nazis took power in Germany. Much more on this subject later.

The League of Nations started a mandate system in the early twentieth century for the purpose of administrating territories that were non-self-governing. This was important to assure that the well-being of its population remained a priority. In 1922, Great Britain was assigned a task by the League to establish a Jewish national home in Palestine. The British granted the Jews and Arabs the right to run their own affairs, but this did not succeed as hoped in that England withdrew from its commitment under Arab pressure, and this resulted in severe land restriction for Jews. In 1947, Great Britain announced it would terminate its mandate over Palestine to take effect on May 15, 1948. The Jewish State of Israel was established the day before. It has flourished but remains under threat from enemies to this day.

ADOLPH HITLER

This sad story now takes its worst turn with the introduction of Adolph Hitler whose vicious anti-Semitism led him to the greatest mass murder in all of modern history—the slaughter of 6 million Jews of all ages. His hatred knew no bounds. What were the roots of this virulence?

He grew up in Vienna Austria, a bastion of anti-Semitism during his formative years. Initially, it was suggested that he watched his mother's death of breast cancer under the care of a Jewish doctor named Eduard Bloch, so he turned his enmity in the doctor's direction expanding it easily to all Jews adding to the anti-Jewish brainwashing he had experienced as a teenager and young man. A recent book written on the subject denies this thesis in reference to Dr. Block.

In the early 1900s a German novelist named Julius Langbehn wrote and described Jews as poison, plague and vermin. He believes that Hitler was merely one of the many Germans influenced by such thinking, and the environment where Hitler lived in Vienna drew him as well as many others toward anti-Semitism. It took the German defeat in World War 1 for Hitler's anti-Semitism to reach extreme levels. He viewed Communists and Jews as one and the same.

When Hitler became chancellor of Germany, a Dutch Communist set fire to the Reichstag building. Hitler immediately stated that, "there will be no mercy shown. Anyone who stands in our way will be butchered." Now that he was Chancellor, Jews and Communists knew that his words were serious, since he now had all the power he needed to control decision making in Germany with an iron fist.

He would start with legislation on German Jews which were geared to severely restrict Jewish life in Germany:

1933

Jewish physicians can no longer be employed in charity services and government service. Jewish attorneys cannot be admitted to the bar. Overcrowded public schools and Universities demand a limit on Jewish students. Naturalized Jews and "undesirables" will have citizenship revoked. Jews will be banned from editorial posts.

1935

Jewish army officers will be expelled from the army.

The Nuremberg Laws defined whether a person was Jewish according to ancestry. Anybody who had three Jewish Grandparents was considered Jewish. If they had three Jewish grandparents, or two grandparents who were religious or married to a Jew, they were considered fully Jewish. They could not have sexual relations with non-Jews. Also Gypsys or blacks could not have sexual relationships with non-Jewish Germans. The Nazis carried these categorizations to the extremes so that 1.5 million people in Germany who never practiced Judaism were considered Jews based upon the fact that they had one or two Jewish grandparents.

1936

Jews may not serve as tax consultants or veterinarians or teachers in public schools

1937

No Jewish children allowed in public schools in Berlin.

1938

Jews may not change their names.

Jews may not be auctioneers, may not be gun merchants, may not change the name of their firm and must disclose all assets in excess of 5,000 Reichmarks.

Jews are banned from health spas.

Female Jews must adopt an additional name "Sara." Male Jews additional name is "Israel."

Regulation of Jewish property transfer of assets to non-Jews established.

Jewish passports must be stamped with J.

Jewish businesses closed.

Freedom of movement is restricted for Jews.

Jews may not keep carrier pigeons.

State contracts with Jews are forbidden.

Jews may not serve as midwives.

1939

Jews must surrender precious metals and stones.

No lottery tickets can be sold to Jews.

As we can see, there was a progressive deterioration of Jewish rights once Hitler took power in Germany.

KRISTALLNACHT

Ernst vom Rath, stationed in Paris, was a German official who was assassinated by a Polish, 17 year old Jew named Herschel Grynszpan. He did this in revenge for his parents expelled from Germany along with thousands of Jews of Polish origin who then all ended up in a refugee camp. This prompted Hitler to seize the moment and order his Storm Troopers to wreak havoc on Germany's Jews. German Propaganda minister, Josef Goebbels then ordered a "revolt" to appear 'spontaneously' against German Jews, described as 'World Jewry,' the perpetrators of the atrocity. Riots against Jews and Jewish owned property started in earnest accompanied by massive damage through the night that would come to be known as Krystallnacht (the night of broken glass). Elements of the German military as well as Hitler Youth members participated in the riots dressed in civilian clothes to make it appear that this was a spontaneous uprising by an enraged citizenry aiming their wrath only on Jews. The German police were instructed to arrest as many young Jews as they could. Thirty thousand Jews were arrested and ended up in Dachau, Sachsenhausen, and Buchenwald. Hundreds died in the camps. Those imprisoned were eventually released under the condition that they leave the country.

The financial crisis emanating from the violence prompted the German government to blame the Jews for the riots and levied a fine of one billion Reichmarks, the equivalent of 400 million US dollars at the time. They confiscated all insurance company payouts the Jew received and added more onerous laws impacting Jews. Most important was the fact that anti-Jewish policy was now put in the hands of the S.S. The passive German population, regarding the events that had taken place, gave the German leaders confidence that they could do whatever they want as regards Jews including making Germany judenrein—free of Jews.

START OF WORLD WAR 2

It is easy to look back through a retrospectoscope, but most historians agree that the seeds of World War 2 started at the end of World War 1 when Germany and Austria-Hungary were crippled by loss of territory and financial sanctions. The German air force was abolished and the army was restricted in is numbers, in essence isolating the country and making them impotent. The Rhineland, that part of Germany west of the Rhine River, was demilitarized.

Chancellor Merkle, the current Chancellor of Germany as of this writing at the end of 2017, is quoted as saying, "The majority had, at the very best, behaved with indifference." She was referring to the emergence of Adolph Hitler on the scene. He was a corporal in World War 1, was injured twice during the war when he served primarily as a message runner, was the recipient of two Iron Crosses, Germany's highest military honor, and most likely because of this distinguished record during the war was retained in the army which had been restricted to no more than 100,000 by the Versailles Treaty that ended World War 1.

Germany, after World War 1 was beset by violence and Communist agitators fighting for control of the country. Hitler's new position in the military was to investigate subversive organizations. In essence he acted as a spy, assigned by the military to clandestinely evaluate these new organizations. He was told to investigate a party known as the German Worker's Party. The word 'worker' in the title was often in Communistic organization titles, therefore Hitler was assigned this task. When he did investigate, he discovered that this party, run by Mr. Anton Drexler, was not Communistic, but indeed was in accord with his own standards of anti-Communism and anti-Semitism. He joined and soon became its new leader. The world would never be the same again from this time forward.

As early as 1919, Hitler is quoted as saying, "The ultimate goal is the removal of the Jews altogether." What the world did not understand was the definition of the word—removal.

He swiftly took control of the party, changed its name to the National Socialist German Workers' Party, or Nazis for short and chose the swastika for its new emblem. A disenfranchised populace embraced Hitler's new party and he won support from the masses seemingly agreeing with his anti-Jewish philosophy. Hitler continuously stressed that the Jews were responsible for Germany's failing economy and political instability. He quickly established a hierarchal governmental scheme with himself at its acme, and when President Paul von Hindenberg died, he established himself as Chancellor—which to him meant dictator. The public supported him, and he attracted many donations in support of his principle thesis that the Jews were responsible for what Germany had just gone through.

Hitler's strong "take no prisoner" leadership style resulted in improving German's potential so that, by the mid 1930's Germany had re-arrived on the European scene with increasing strength while the rest of Europe's countries were in a weakened state. This dominance did not go unnoticed by Hitler who proceeded to take advantage of this status. By 1939, he became emboldened and denounced the Treaty of Versailles which ended World War 1.

The domination of Europe, the first step in what he envisioned for Germany, started in earnest. In his mind was complete domination, which probably meant war; a war of revenge. The Spanish Civil war was over; a war in which Hitler participated. He had the courage to annex Austria, he reoccupied the Sudetenland in defiance of the Versailles treaty and he took over parts of Czechoslovakia. He did this all with boldness and threats while the rest of Europe attempted appeasement rather than confront him head on. The next attempt on Hitler's schedule was to "repair" relationships with Poland while Britain and France stood by anxiously. Needless to say this attempt failed Hitler's testing procedure, and he invaded Poland with overwhelming force that Hitler had built up in spite of the Treaty of Versailles restrictions. Two days later, World War 2 was unleashed when Britain and France declared war on Germany.

Unbeknownst to the world—and the Jews—the Jews fate was sealed.

WORLD WAR 2 AND THE JEW

In the Greek language, Holocaust means "sacrifice by fire" a fancy, generalized statement for what the holocaust really was; the killing by gun, hanging, starvation, bayonet, gassing and other means of death. Jews, Gypsys, Poles, Slavs, Russians, those disabled physically or mentally, Communists, Socialists, homosexuals were easy targets; the ends of their lives justified because they were all inferiors that were better off dead. The Jews were the great majority of the victims—six million by actual count. Their death was necessary because, according to the Nazis, the Jews wanted to control the world. That, of course, could not be allowed to happen because an important responsibility such as world leadership must be left to the most superior beings—the Nazis led by Adolph Hitler. This is the philosophy followed all the way to the bitter end when Hitler and his mistress ended their lives together in 1945.

Before Hitler assumed power in Germany in 1933, after fourteen years of what I could only describe as life and death political infighting in the struggle for power, Hitler came through as the winner. Others usually did not survive because they would die suddenly, or of unusual circumstances.

Through this period of fourteen years there were over nine million Jews living in Europe. They lived in Germany and many other countries, most of which were soon to be controlled by the Nazi hordes. By the time the war was over in 1945, the Nazis and their buddies killed two thirds of all European Jews as part of their "Final Solution." The others involved in this genocide were 200,000 Gypsys, 200,000 mentally and physically disabled persons, two million plus Soviet prisoners of war, and many Polish citizens involved in forced labor duties, many of whom died.

The killing of so many people necessitated industrial-like efficiency. With this in mind, the Nazis constructed many concentration camps to house and kill their victims. Also constructed were ghettos where Jews were housed awaiting death.

Those involved in the Russian invasion during the war included the German Einsatsgruppen (mobile killing units). They had a clear responsibility—kill Jews and other undesirables. They succeeded admirably, killing at least one million Jews and others including government officials, Communist party officials, and gypsies often by gassing.

Seven hundred thousand Jewish survivors at the end of the war managed, over time, to get to Israel where they took up residence.

Hitler and his mistress committed suicide rather than be captured.

Following this horrible war, there were very many less Jewish communities in Europe. Sixty million people were killed during the war, ten percent, or six million were Jews slaughtered by Nazis in the holocaust.

PART THREE

ANTI-SEMITISM

WHO TO HATE AND KILL

Jew hating has been with us for many centuries. The main causes are religiously based, but also anti-Semitism has political, economic, social, cultural, and racial roots.

In ancient Rome, Jewish religious and cultural practices were tolerated until Constantine, the first Christian Roman Emperor, fueled anti-Jewish prejudice.

Christianity began its existence as a sect of Judaism rather than a separate religion. For Christians, Jesus was the Messiah, or son of God. For Jews, Jesus was a mortal man. This difference was reflected in the New Testament written in the first century A.D., a treatise interpreted as being a rejection of Judaism's beliefs. By the second century, many Christians turned against Judaism even though it was Christianity's parent religion. Early Christian thinkers accused Jews of being responsible for turning Jesus Christ, one of their own, over to Pontius Pilot and supported his crucifixion. This 'God Murder' is said to have condemned the Jews to wander the earth forever. In addition, Christians objected to the declaration made in the Torah as well as in rabbinical scripture that "Jews are a holy people whom God has chosen to be his treasured people from all the nations that are on the face of the earth." This statement, understood by many to be blasphemous and arrogant, suggested that Jews considered themselves superior to those not Jewish. By the middle ages, persecution and harassment became the plight of Jews causing most of them to withdraw within themselves and avoid non-Jews. This only maximized their self-isolation interpreted by many to mean that Jews felt themselves superior to Christians.

Martin Luther tried to convert the Jews, but when they did not profess interest in his entreaties, he is quoted as saying, "Let the magistrates burn their synagogues and let whatever escapes be covered with sand and mud. Let them be forced to work, and if this avails nothing we will be compelled to expel them like dogs."

In distant pre-scientific times, disastrous and unexpected events were considered to be the result of divine intervention, witchcraft, superstition, black magic, or Jews. Without scientific explanation available, Jews were often considered the cause of these unusual events and natural disasters, so they suffered the consequences including death in many instances. This fate alleviated as time brought scientific advances to the world, but enough anti-Semitism prevailed to curse Jews even to this day.

Long before Adolph Hitler and the Nazis arrived on the scene, anti-Jewish thinking was rampant not just in Germany but in most of Europe's population. There was one branch of Judaism at that time, the orthodox, very separate and distinct from Christianity with entirely foreign religious dress and practices. Jews were an "ancient people" with a reverence for learning stretching back to even before the ancient Greek and Roman republics, and when they entered into Europe during the middle ages, the contrast between them and the Europeans was stark in all religious and cultural aspects.

Jews principally abided by the Hebrew Bible (Old Testament) consisting of five books of Moses given to them by God on Mount Sinai. The Hebrew bible, also known as the Torah, is in the form of a scroll made from kosher animal parchment. Ancient tradition tells Jews that the Torah existed in Heaven before the world was created, but others have different interpretations making for fine philosophical arguments during Saturday morning Torah sessions with the rabbi and his parishioners. I say his, because female rabbis represent a modern day advance; there were none in ancient times.

Prior to and in the early 1800's the orthodox Jews kept to themselves. Since Jews were viewed as foreigners by non-Jewish citizens, tensions prevailed. This made for a volatile mixture exacerbating anti-Semitism that would culminate in violence leading eventually to the Holocaust of World War II. As I write this book in the year 2017-18, anti-Semitism has continued increasing throughout the world.

By the mid nineteenth century the orthodoxy of the Jewish religion began to change in Europe. A reform and conservative form of Judaism evolved and much of Germany, especially Berlin, began to assimilate Jews into the culture so that the period around the late 1800's and early nineteen hundreds began to be considered a "golden era" for German Jews. In 1900 there were approximately 587,000 Jews in Germany representing 1.04 percent of the German population.

Before the 1800's, autocratic German leaders including the Prussian King subjected Jews to discriminatory laws such as excess taxes and limits on family size. Jews were prevented from holding political office and were restricted from certain professions. Other leaders, including Napoleon Bonaparte, completely emancipated Jews. As the world moved into a period of rapid industrialization during the 1800's, conditions for Jews improved giving them more opportunity to make an impact in the major professions. Anti-Semitism did not die however, and as German unification expanded from its various nation states, and Theodor Herzl founded Zionism calling for the establishment of a Zionist State in Palestine, these dual effects strengthened long-lasting conspiracy theories involving a Jewish plot to control the world. The future would see this theory persist, become amplified and lead to disaster for Europe's Jews.

Underpinning this development was the fact that Germany in the mid 1800's was not a single nation, but was a patchwork of many kingdoms; a concept opposed by German nationalists who wanted one unified nation to compete on Europe's stage with the likes of Russia, Great Britain, and France. Who better to blame for the nationalist's failure to implement their goal than the Jews who were also trying to unify.

This Jewish unification was viewed by non-Jews as a world-wide Jewish conspiracy theory and it evolved not only in Germany, but also in France where anti-Jewish hatred mushroomed from all sides of the French political spectrum: religious Christian groups condemned Jews on religious grounds while Socialists condemned Jews for having a major impact on business and finance.

An example of the intensity of French anti-Semitism is the Dreyfus affair in 1894: a Jewish French military officer was accused falsely of bringing French military secrets to the Germans. After Dreyfus languished two years in prison on Devil's Island, Emil Zola, a famous French writer, exposed the false charges and Dreyfus was released and returned to military service.

The worst anti-Semitism of the time, however, evolved in Russia. The Russian and Eastern European Jewish population of five million was the largest in Europe. Under Czar Alexander II, the Jews experienced freedoms that allowed many of them a comfortable middle-class life. Alexander's reward for this compassionate accomplishment was his assassination. The new Czar, Alexander III, levied many restrictions on Jews; pogroms swept the country killing Jews in ever increasing numbers and resulted in a Jewish exodus. This was the time when my infant mother and four-year-old father and their parents fled to the United States.

The next Czar, Nicholas II, a rabid anti-Semite, enhanced Jewish restrictions in Russia. Nicholas and his entire family were eventually murdered by Socialist (Communist) revolutionaries in 1918. Following this Communist takeover, Russia and surrounding countries would become known as the Union of Soviet Socialist Republics, a collection of nations controlled by Russia.

Nicholas' secret police (Ochrana) developed their famous forgery, the Protocols of the Learned Elders of Zion, documenting the so-called 'Jewish Conspiracy to rule the world,' which Adolph Hitler would amplify years later. The Protocols have as their ancient origin the anti-Semitism engendered by the falsehood that Jews, by poisoning the wells, caused the plagues that decimated Western Europe in medieval times. Millions died, including Jews, many of whom were burned alive in their homes by the angry non-Jewish population. This was not the only libelous anti-Jewish assertion in the distant past. Word spread that Jews used the blood of Christian children to make their leavened bread (matzos) for the Passover Jewish holiday celebrating liberation from ancient Egyptian enslavement. These twin assertions made life for western European Jews impossible, thus forcing them to flee to Poland where a Polish King who happened to have a Jewish girlfriend welcomed them. This exodus explains the eventual major Jewish population increase in Poland setting the stage for a future German dictator (Adolph Hitler) to zero in and attempt to finish the job, left undone by his predecessors.

In the 1890's, anti-Semitism was primarily a French and Eastern European phenomenon. The above mentioned Dreyfus affair and the well-known pogroms in Poland and Russia that prompted my grandparents flight to the United States was not part of German culture. Jews in Germany enjoyed unfettered business penetration, excellent assimilation, social and religious freedom, and preeminence in the professions. It was only in the civil service and military where they were prevented assimilation. In contrast, however, prior to the 1890's, Germany did persecute socialists and Catholics with some governmental support, but even though there were German anti-Semites in the late 1800's and early 1900's, they had no intra-governmental or political traction. This raises an intriguing question. How did Germany, a relative haven for Jews in the 1890's, evolve into the master planning agent for the destruction of World Jewry in less than forty years?

Adolph Hitler, in his rise to power in Germany, utilized two principle methods in his efforts to bring the German citizens to his way of thinking. The first approach was anti-Semitism, a two-thousand year old phenomenon. He added to Jew hating by bringing others into the mix; specifically Gypsies and Slavs.

Gypsies were wandering people of Europe who originated in Northern India and arrived in Europe during the ninth century. They have been persecuted for much of their existence. They were convenient scapegoats easily added by Hitler to a list of people to hate because they lived in Eastern Europe, an area that Hitler coveted. Hitler would use this fact to invent the fiction that Slavs were untermenschen (inferiors) who must be done away with so as to provide lebensraum (living space) for the German race of superior beings. This was another fiction Hitler used to infect the minds of his citizens, thus offering less opposition to his delusional thinking. To the detriment of the entire world he slowly and inexorably succeeded, paving the way to World War II and the death of 60,000,000 human beings including 6,000,000 Jews deliberately killed.

EPILOGUE

For the reader:

Epilogue printed by permission of the United States Department of State; world-wide anti-Semitism approximately sixty years after the end of World War 2.

September27, 2016

Dear Sheldon:

Information on the Department of State's website is in the public domain and may be copied and distributed without permission, unless a copyright is indicated. If a copyright is indicated, for example on a photo, graphic or other material, permission to copy these materials must be obtained from the original source. For photos without captions or with only partial captions, hold your cursor over the photo to view the "alt tag" for any copyright information.

Please note that the U.S. Government has an international copyright on Country Commercial Guides. Generally, U.S. Government materials are considered in the public domain unless otherwise specified as copyrighted.

Thank you for contacting the U.S. Department of State, Bureau of Public Affairs Office of Public engagement.

Anti-Semitism has plagued the world for centuries. Taken to its most far-reaching and violent extreme, the Holocaust, anti-Semitism resulted in the deaths of millions of Jews and the suffering of countless others. Subtler, less vile forms of anti-Semitism have disrupted lives, decimated religious communities, created social and political cleavages, and complicated relations between countries as well as the work of international organizations. For an increasingly interdependent world, anti-Semitism is an intolerable burden.

The increasing frequency and severity of anti-Semitic incidents since the start of the 21st century, particularly in Europe, has compelled the international community to focus on anti-Semitism with renewed vigor. Attacks on individual Jews and on Jewish properties occurred in the immediate post World War II period, but decreased over time and were primarily linked to vandalism and criminal activity. In recent years, incidents have been more targeted in nature with perpetrators appearing to have the specific intent to attack Jews and Judaism. These attacks have disrupted the sense of safety and well-being of Jewish communities.

The definition of anti-Semitism has been the focus of innumerable discussions and studies. While there is no universally accepted definition, there is a generally clear understanding of what the term encompasses.

For the purposes of this report, anti-Semitism is considered to be hatred toward Jews—individually and as a group—that can be attributed to the Jewish religion and/or ethnicity. An important issue is the distinction between legitimate criticism of policies and practices of the State of Israel, and commentary that assumes an anti-Semitic character. The demonization of Israel, or vilification of Israeli leaders, sometimes through comparisons with Nazi leaders, and through the use of Nazi symbols to caricature them, indicates an anti-Semitic bias rather than a valid criticism of policy concerning a controversial issue.

Global anti-Semitism in recent years has had four main sources:

- Traditional anti-Jewish prejudice that has pervaded Europe and some countries in other parts of the world for centuries. This includes ultra-nationalists and others who assert that the Jewish community controls governments, the media, international business, and the financial world.
- Strong anti-Israel sentiment that crosses the line between objective criticism of Israeli policies and anti-Semitism.
- Anti-Jewish sentiment expressed by some in Europe's growing Muslim population, based on longstanding antipathy toward both

Israel and Jews, as well as Muslim opposition to developments in Israel and the occupied territories, and more recently in Iraq.

- Criticism of both the United States and globalization that spills over to Israel, and to Jews in general who are identified with both.

II. Harassment, Vandalism and Physical Violence

Europe and Eurasia

Anti-Semitism in Europe increased significantly in recent years. At the same time it should be noted that many European countries have comprehensive reporting systems that record incidents more completely than is possible in other countries. Because of this significant difference in reporting systems, it is not possible to make direct comparisons between countries or geographic regions. Beginning in 2000, verbal attacks directed against Jews increased while incidents of vandalism (e.g. graffiti, fire bombings of Jewish schools, desecration of synagogues and cemeteries) surged. Physical assaults including beatings, stabbings and other violence against Jews in Europe increased markedly, in a number of cases resulting in serious injury and even death. Also troubling is a bias that spills over into anti-Semitism in some of the left-of-center press and among some intellectuals.

The disturbing rise of anti-Semitic intimidation and incidents is widespread throughout Europe, although with significant variations in the number of cases and the accuracy of reporting. European governments in most countries now view anti-Semitism as a serious problem for their societies and demonstrate a greater willingness to address the issue. The Vienna-based European Union Monitoring Center (EUMC), for 2002 and 2003, identified France, Germany, the United Kingdom, Belgium, and The Netherlands as EU member countries with notable increases in incidents. As these nations keep reliable and comprehensive statistics on anti-Semitic acts, and are engaged in combating anti-Semitism, their data was readily available to the EUMC. Governments and leading public figures condemned the violence, passed new legislation, and mounted positive law enforcement and educational efforts.

In Western Europe, traditional far-right groups still account for a significant proportion of the attacks against Jews and Jewish properties;

disadvantaged and disaffected Muslim youths increasingly were responsible for most of the other incidents. This trend appears likely to persist as the number of Muslims in Europe continues to grow while their level of education and economic prospects remain limited.

In Eastern Europe, with a much smaller Muslim population, skinheads and others members of the radical political fringe were responsible for most anti-Semitic incidents. Anti-Semitism remained a serious problem in Russia and Belarus, and elsewhere in the former Soviet Union, with most incidents carried out by ultra-nationalist and other far-right elements. The stereotype of Jews as manipulators of the global economy continues to provide fertile ground for anti-Semitic aggression.

Holocaust and tolerance education as well as teacher training provide a potential long-term solution to anti-Semitism; however, the problem is still rapidly outpacing the solution. At the end of 2003, and continuing into this year, some Jews, especially in Europe, faced the dilemma either of hiding their identity or facing harassment and sometimes even serious bodily injury and death. The heavy psychological toll in this increasingly difficult environment should not be overlooked or underestimated.

Middle East

Jews left the countries of the Middle East and North Africa in large numbers near the mid-point of the last century as their situation became increasingly precarious. This trend continues. Today few remain, and few incidents involving the remaining members of the Jewish community have been reported. Nonetheless, Syria condoned and, in some cases, even supported through radio, television programming, news articles, and other mass media the export of a virulent domestic anti-Semitism. The official and state-supported media's anti-Zionist propaganda frequently adopts the terminology and symbols of the Holocaust to demonize Israel and its leaders. This rhetoric often crosses the line separating the legitimate criticism of Israel and its policies to become anti-Semitic vilification posing as legitimate political commentary. At the same time, Holocaust denial and Holocaust minimization efforts find increasingly overt acceptance as sanctioned historical discourse in a number of Middle Eastern countries.

Other Regions

The problem of anti-Semitism is not only significant in Europe and in the Middle East, but there are also worrying expressions of it elsewhere. For example, in Pakistan, a country without a Jewish community, anti-Semitic sentiment fanned by anti-Semitic articles in the press is widespread. This reflects the more recent phenomenon of anti-Semitism appearing in countries where historically or currently there are few or even no Jews.

Elsewhere, in Australia, the level of intimidation and attacks against Jews and Jewish property and anti-Zionist and anti-Semitic rhetoric decreased somewhat over the past year. This year, New Zealand experienced several desecrations of Jewish tombstones and other incidents. In the Americas, in addition to manifestations of anti-Semitism in the United States, Canada experienced a significant increase in attacks against Jews and Jewish property. There were notable anti-Semitic incidents in Argentina and isolated incidents in a number of other Latin American countries.

III. Media

The proliferation of media outlets (television, radio, print media and the internet) has vastly increased the opportunity for purveyors of anti-Semitic material to spread their propaganda unhindered. Anti-hate laws provide some protection, but freedom of expression safeguards in many western countries limited the preventive measures that governments could take. Satellite television programming easily shifts from one provider to another and Internet offerings cross international borders with few or no impediments.

In June, the Organization for Security and Cooperation in Europe (OSCE) organized a separate meeting in Paris dealing with intolerance on the Internet, and subsequently approved a decision on "Promoting Tolerance and Media Freedom on the Internet." The decision is prescriptive in nature and carefully caveated to avoid conflict with the varied legal systems within the countries of the OSCE. It calls upon Participating States to investigate and fully prosecute criminal threats of violence based on anti-Semitic and other intolerance on the Internet, as well as to establish programs to educate children about hate speech and other forms of bias.

Critics of Israel frequently use anti-Semitic cartoons depicting anti-Jewish images and caricatures to attack the State of Israel and its policies, as well as Jewish communities and others who support Israel. These media attacks can lack any pretext of balance or even factual basis and focus on the demonization of Israel. The United States is frequently included as a target of such attacks, which often assert that U.S. foreign policy is made in Israel or that Jews control the media and financial markets in the United States and the rest of the world. During the 2004 United States presidential campaign, the Arab press ran numerous cartoons closely identifying both of the major American political parties with Israel and with Israeli Prime Minister Sharon.

"The Protocols of the Elders of Zion," a text debunked many years ago as a fraud perpetrated by Czarist intelligence agents, continued to appear in the Middle East media, not as a hoax, but as established fact. Government-sponsored television in Syria ran lengthy serials based on the Protocols. The presentations emphasized blood libel and the alleged control by the Jewish community of international finance. The clear purpose of the programs was to incite hatred of Jews and of Israel. Copies of the Protocols and other similar anti-Semitic forgeries were readily available in Middle Eastern countries, former Soviet republics and elsewhere. Similarly, allegations that Jews were behind the 9/11 attacks were widely disseminated.

In November 2004, Al-Manar, the Lebanon-based television network controlled by Hizballah featuring blatantly anti-Semitic material, obtained a limited 1-year satellite broadcast license from the French authorities. This was revoked shortly thereafter due to Al-Manar's continued transmission of anti-Semitic material. Al-Manar is now off the air in France. Other Middle East networks with questionable content, such as Al-Jazeerah and Al-Arrabiya, maintain their French broadcast licenses.

IV. Actions by Governments

In Europe and other geographic regions, many governments became increasingly aware of the threat presented by anti-Semitism and spoke out against it. Some took effective measures to combat it with several countries, including France, Belgium, and Germany, now providing enhanced protection for members of the Jewish community and Jewish properties.

For the most part, the police response to anti-Semitic incidents was uneven. Most law enforcement officials are not specifically trained to deal with hate crimes, particularly anti-Semitic hate crimes. Police sometimes dismissed such crimes as hooliganism or petty crime, rather than attacks against Jews because of their ethnicity or religion, or because the assailants identified the victims with the actions of the State of Israel.

In countries where anti-Semitism is a serious problem, specialized training for police and members of the judiciary remains a pressing need. Many nations still do not have hate crime laws that address anti-Semitic and other intolerance-related crimes. In some instances where such laws already exist, stronger enforcement is needed.

V. Multilateral Action

Anti-Semitism is a global problem that requires a coordinated multinational approach. Thus far, the most effective vehicle for international cooperation has been the OSCE, comprised of 55 participating states from Europe, Eurasia and North America plus Mediterranean and Asian partners for cooperation. The OSCE organized two groundbreaking conferences on anti-Semitism--in June 2003, in Vienna and in April 2004, in Berlin. These were the first international conferences to focus high-level political attention solely on the problem of anti-Semitism. The Vienna Conference identified anti-Semitism as a human rights issue.

OSCE Foreign Ministers gave further high-level political acknowledgment to the seriousness of anti-Semitism at their December 2003 meeting in Maastricht. There they took the formal decision to spotlight the need to combat anti-Semitism by deciding to task the OSCE's Office of Democratic Institutions and Human Rights (ODIHR) to serve as a collection point for hate crimes information. ODIHR is now working with OSCE member states to collect information on hate crimes legislation and to promote "best practices" in the areas of law enforcement, combating hate crimes, and education. ODIHR established a Program on Tolerance and Non-Discrimination and now has an advisor to deal exclusively with the issue.

At their December 2004 meeting in Sofia, OSCE Foreign Ministers welcomed the Chair-in-Office's decision to appoint three special representatives for tolerance issues, including a special representative for anti-Semitism, to work with member states on implementing specific commitments to fight anti-Semitism. In addition, the Foreign Ministers accepted the Spanish Government's offer to host a third anti-Semitism conference in June 2005 in Cordoba.

The United Nations also took important measures in the fight against anti-Semitism. One was a June 2004 seminar on anti-Semitism hosted by Secretary General Kofi Annan. Another measure was a resolution of the United Nations Third Committee in November 2004, which called for the elimination of all forms of religious intolerance, explicitly including anti-Semitism.

Education remains a potentially potent antidote for anti-Semitism and other forms of intolerance. Following the first Stockholm Conference in 1998, convoked out of concern for the decreasing level of knowledge of the Holocaust particularly among the younger generation, Sweden, the United Kingdom and the United States decided to address the issue collaboratively. The Task Force for International Cooperation on Holocaust Education, Remembrance, and Research (ITF) emerged from this initial effort.

Today the ITF, an informal international organization operating on the basis of consensus, and without a bureaucracy, consists of 20 countries. ITF member states agree to commit themselves to the Declaration of the Stockholm International Forum on the Holocaust and to its implementation. Current members of the ITF include Argentina, Austria, Czech Republic, Denmark, France, Germany, Hungary, Israel, Italy, Latvia, Lithuania, Luxembourg, the Netherlands, Norway, Poland, Romania, Sweden, Switzerland, United Kingdom, and the United States. In addition, four other countries (Croatia, Estonia, Greece, Slovakia) maintain a liaison relationship with the ITF.

VI. U.S. Government Actions to Monitor and Combat Anti-Semitism

The U.S. Government is committed to monitoring and combating anti-Semitism throughout the world as an important human rights and religious issue. President Bush said when he signed the Global

Anti-Semitism Review Act on October 16, 2004, "Defending freedom also means disrupting the evil of anti-Semitism."

Annually, the U.S. Department of State publishes the International Religious Freedom Report and the Country Reports on Human Rights Practices. Both detail incidents and trends of anti-Semitism worldwide. The State Department's instructions to U.S. Embassies for the 2004 Country Reports on Human Rights Practices explicitly required them to describe acts of violence against Jews and Jewish properties, as well as actions governments are taking to prevent this form of bigotry and prejudice.

In multilateral fora, the Department of State called for recognition of the rise of anti-Semitism and the development of specific measures to address it. The Department played a leading role in reaching agreement in the OSCE to hold the two conferences on combating anti-Semitism noted above in Section V. Former New York City Mayors Rudolph Giuliani and Edward Koch led the United States delegations to the conferences in Vienna and Berlin, respectively. Each brought a wealth of knowledge and experience in fostering respect for minorities in multicultural communities. Key NGOs worked productively with the Department to prepare for these conferences. In his address to the Berlin Conference, Secretary Powell said: "We must not permit anti-Semitic crimes to be shrugged off as inevitable side effects of inter-ethnic conflicts. Political disagreements do not justify physical assaults against Jews in our streets, the destruction of Jewish schools, or the desecration of synagogues and cemeteries. There is no justification for anti-Semitism." At the United Nations, the United States has supported resolutions condemning anti-Semitism both at the General Assembly and at the UN Commission on Human Rights.

An important lesson of the Holocaust is that bigotry and intolerance can lead to future atrocities and genocides if not addressed forcefully by governments and other sectors of society. The United States is committed to working bilaterally to promote efforts with other governments to arrest and roll back the increase in anti-Semitism. President Bush affirmed that commitment during his visit to Auschwitz-Birkenau in 2003, stating: "This site is a sobering reminder that when we find anti-Semitism, whether it be in Europe, in America or anywhere else, mankind must come together to fight such dark impulses."

U.S. Embassies implement this commitment by speaking out against anti-Semitic acts and hate crimes. Ambassadors and other embassy officers work with local Jewish communities to encourage prompt law enforcement action against hate crimes. In Turkey, the U.S. Embassy worked closely with the Jewish community following the November 2003 bombing of the Neve Shalom Synagogue. In the Middle East, our embassies have protested to host governments against practices that have allowed their institutions to promote anti-Semitism, such as the heavily watched television series Rider Without a Horse and Diaspora that respectively promoted the canard of the blood libel, and "The Protocols of Elders of Zion." U.S. bilateral demarches were effective in specific instances, but more remains to be done to encourage national leaders to speak out forcefully against anti-Semitism and in support of respectful, tolerant societies.

Building on the success achieved to date, the Department of State is accelerating its efforts with its partners globally to improve both monitoring and combating anti-Semitism in three specific areas: education, legislation, and law enforcement. The Department will continue to promote the development of Holocaust education curricula and teacher training programs. A successful program in this area has been summer teacher training partially funded through U.S. Embassies in cooperation with the Association of American Holocaust Organizations (AHO) and the United States Holocaust Memorial Museum (USHMM). At the October 2004 OSCE Human Dimension Meeting, the United States and France hosted a seminar on methodologies for teaching the Holocaust in multicultural societies. The United States also supports the work of NGOs in promoting educational programs abroad, in part based on successful seminars in the United States that teach respect for individuals and minority groups. Additionally, the U.S. State Department has supported efforts to promote tolerance in the Saudi educational system including by sponsoring the travel of religious educators to the United States to examine interreligious education.

The roots of anti-Semitism run deep and the United States does not underestimate the difficulty of reversing the recent resurgence of this ancient scourge. The legislative and executive branches, together with NGOs, constitute an important partnership in continuing the vital effort to find creative ways to monitor, contain, and finally stop anti-Semitism.

Anti-Semitism in Europe and Eurasia

Anti-Semitism was a widely dispersed problem in the region, although the severity and scope of abuses varied significantly among individual countries. During the reporting period, the most serious incidents of anti-Semitism—beatings and other physical abuses—occurred in 12 countries. Verbal harassment was reported in 28 countries, while desecration of cemeteries and synagogues was reported in 30 countries. The recent rise in anti-Jewish acts and sentiments in Western Europe was often influenced by Middle Eastern events or conflated with anti-Israeli views.

In 16 countries in the Europe and Eurasia region, there were few or no reported anti-Semitic incidents in recent years. This report is not intended as a comprehensive description of all incidents, but focuses on illustrative or particularly egregious cases. In the European context, the number of incidents reported in some countries reflects not only the depth of the problem, but also the thorough reporting on anti-Semitism by active civil societies, religious representatives, and governments themselves. As a result, there is sometimes an imbalance in the scope of reporting in the country narratives below.

Government responses have varied as well. Many European governments effectively prosecute those who perpetrate or incite anti-Semitic attacks or harassment, while others include officials who themselves make anti-Semitic statements or discriminate against Jews. Many European leaders have condemned anti-Semitism and called for tolerance, and several countries have joined the Council of Europe in declaring a Holocaust Memorial Day. In a June 2003 anti-Semitism conference, the Organization for Security and Cooperation in Europe (OSCE) called on member states to reaffirm their commitments to condemn racial and ethnic hatred, including anti-Semitism, and to undertake effective follow-up plans of action to demonstrate these commitments in practice. In response, some countries have already implemented action plans.

Armenia

The Jewish community reported several incidents of verbal harassment during the reporting period. The director of ALM TV frequently made anti-Semitic remarks on the air, and the Union of Armenian Aryans, a small, ultranationalist group, called for the country to be "purified" of Jews and Yezidis.

On September 17, offices of the Jewish community in Yerevan received a message that vandals had damaged the local memorial to the victims of the Holocaust. Several photographs of the memorial were taken and the vandalism was immediately reported to the local police, the Ministry of Religious Affairs, and the government-owned television channel. A television crew arrived at the site together with an official from the Jewish community in Yerevan and to their surprise discovered that the memorial had been wiped clean, apparently by the park guard.

In May, Jewish groups complained to several government authorities about the distribution and importation of hate literature. Each government agency they contacted responded that the literature was in apparent violation of the "Law on Distributing Literature Inflaming National Hatred" and suggested they press formal charges with the Prosecutor General's office. Jewish leaders have not yet decided whether to press charges.

Austria

The Austrian NGO Forum gegen Antisemitismus (the Forum against Anti-Semitism, FGA) reported five physical attacks during the reporting period and eight in 2003. On July 30, 2003, according to the Coordination Forum, several unidentified persons beat an Orthodox Jew. The man was attacked from behind and beaten with belts. The assailants fled the scene and have not been arrested or identified. The victim was hospitalized suffering from bruises but was fully conscious. In a separate incident, an unknown assailant attacked two Orthodox Jews, one of whom was injured. In another incident, skinheads attacked the vice-director of a Jewish school in Vienna with a beer bottle, leaving the victim with injuries.

FGA also recorded 122 anti-Semitic incidents in the first 11 months of the year and 134 in 2003. The incidents included name-calling, graffiti/defacement, threatening letters, anti-Semitic Internet postings, property damage, vilifying letters and telephone calls, and physical attacks. The European Union's Monitoring Center on Racism and Xenophobia declared that anti-Semitism in the country is characterized by diffuse and traditional anti-Semitic stereotypes rather than by acts of physical aggression.

On May 24, the Coordination Forum reported that a letter with anti-Semitic and xenophobic contents was received at the Jewish Community Building in Vienna.

On June 1, in Villach, according to the Anti-Defamation League (ADL), vandals smashed a memorial honoring Holocaust victims in southern Austria. The memorial consisted of 17 glass plates engraved with the names of 108 local Holocaust victims. Vandals previously damaged the memorial in March 2003.

On October 24, the Coordination Forum reported that anti-Semitic comments were made at a neo-Nazi convention in the Province of Klagenfurt. Local authorities are examining whether holding the convention was a violation of the law.

On November 25, 2003, according to the Coordination Forum, an anonymous telephone call was received at the Jewish school in Vienna; the caller said: "There is a bomb in the school." He repeated the announcement and hung up. The school was evacuated and police conducted a search of the premises, but found nothing.

The law prohibits any racially motivated or anti-Semitic propaganda, and as a result, anti-Jewish propaganda does not exist in government publications. Nongovernmental media that seek to promote anti-Semitism cannot do so openly, but attempt to use veiled language that is nevertheless clearly understood by most citizens. Such groups are under close observation by the Government (especially the Bureau for Protection of the Constitution) and by private anti-discrimination groups. The Documentation Center of Austrian Resistance (DOEW) monitors the activities and publications of extreme right-wing groups and considers the following to contain revisionist and extremist viewpoints: Aula, Kommentare zur Zeitgeschehen, Arbeitsgemeinschaft fuer demokratische Politik (AFP), Huttenbriefe-Deutsches Kulturwerk Europaeischen Geistes (DKEG)/Deutsche Kulturgemeinschaft (DKG), Die Kameradschaft (Kameradschaft IV (K IV)), Fakten (published by "Die Kritischen Demokraten"), Der Eckart (Oesterreichische Landsmannschaft (OELM)), PNO-Nachrichten (Partei Neue Ordnung (PNO)), Top Secret - Phoenix, Die Umwelt, and Halt.

The 1947 Law against Neo-Nazi Activity ("Verbotsgesetz") prohibits any form of neo-Nazism and anti-Semitism and any type of activity in the spirit of National Socialism. In particular, it bans National Socialist or neo-Nazi organizations, and prohibits incitement to neo-Nazi activity, as well as the glorification or praise of National Socialist ideology. It also prohibits public denial, belittlement, approval, or justification of National Socialist crimes, including the Holocaust. The Criminal Code prohibits public incitement to hostile acts, insult, or contempt against a church or religious society, or public incitement against a group based on race, nationality, or ethnicity, if that incitement could pose a danger to the public order. The Government strictly enforces its anti-neo-Nazi legislation and provides police protection for Jewish community institutions. During the reporting period, the country implemented the EU anti-discrimination guidelines.

The Ministry of the Interior's Internet hotline for reporting National Socialist activity received 140 reports of right-wing extremist activity, particularly in connection with the Internet.

The FGA reported that cooperation with the police and federal and regional authorities is very good. The FGA also stated that leading newspapers have been very responsive to requests to remove anti-Semitic postings on their online forum pages.

The Government recognized the Jewish faith community as one of 13 religious societies under an 1874 law. This had wide-ranging implications, such as providing the authority to participate in the mandatory church contributions program, to provide religious instruction in public schools, and to bring religious workers into the country to act as ministers, missionaries, or teachers. The Government also provided financial support to religious teachers affiliated with religious societies at both public and private schools.

Holocaust education was generally taught as part of history instruction, but also was featured in other subjects under the heading "political education (civics)." Religious education classes were another forum for teaching the tenets of different religions and overall tolerance.

Special teacher training seminars were available on the subject of Holocaust education. The Education Ministry also ran a program through which Holocaust survivors talked to school classes about National Socialism and the Holocaust.

One example of a large-scale Holocaust education project was the "Letters to the Stars" in 2003, in which more than 15,000 students participated. Students chose a Holocaust victim who had lived in their neighborhood, did research on the person's life, and then wrote a letter to that victim. The letters were released on balloons during a ceremony on May 5.

Azerbaijan

The Mountain Jewish Community has resided in the country for 2,700 years; the Ashkenazi Jews have been present for more than 100 years.

Cases of prejudice and discrimination against Jews in the country were very limited, and in the few instances of anti-Semitic activity the Government has been quick to respond. There was only one reported incident during the period covered by this report. In April, the Lubavitch community received an anonymous letter containing threats during the observance of Passover. The police and military responded by blocking and securing Jewish places of worship to ensure the peaceful observance of the Passover holiday. The subsequent investigation revealed that a member of a small radical Islamic group wrote the letter, resulting in his conviction and imprisonment.

The Government does not condone or tolerate persecution of Jews by any party. No laws specifically address anti-Semitism.

Belarus

According to the Union of Councils for Jews in the Former Soviet Union (UCSJ), in 2003 memorials in Minsk and Lida commemorating victims of genocide were vandalized. During the reporting period, vandalism at Jewish cemeteries occurred in Bobruisk and Tcherven and at a Holocaust memorial in Brest. The local authorities refused to react to these incidents. The Prosecutor's office and the Committee for State Security (KGB) did nothing to investigate groups of skinheads and Russian National Unity (RNE), which functioned openly in Minsk, Grodno, Gomel, Vitebsk, and Polotsk. The RNE was banned in the country.

According to Jewish leaders, cases of vandalism decreased during the reporting period. Authorities initiated investigations, but in the past 15 years no vandals have been fined or jailed. The police failed to prosecute suspects to the fullest extent of the law. The Government restored monuments and memorials that were vandalized. The Government also allowed the erection of a memorial to Jews killed by Soviet security forces at Kurapaty.

On August 18, the Ministry of Foreign Affairs notified the local chapter of the UCSJ that it would not be reregistered, because the chapter submitted some documents late. The UCSJ is one of the primary Jewish human rights organizations in the country and previously worked with the Ministry of Education to provide material on the Holocaust.

Despite a May 2003 order by the Prosecutor General and the Ministry of Information to terminate distribution of the anti-Semitic and xenophobic newspaper Russki Vestnik, distribution of the newspaper resumed in February through the government-distribution agency Belzoyuzprechat. Sales of similar literature continued throughout the year in government-owned buildings, in stores, and at events affiliated with the Belarusian Orthodox Church (BOC). Anti-Semitic and Russian ultranationalistic literature continued to be sold at Pravoslavnaya Kniga (Orthodox Bookstore), a store operated by Orthodox Initiative that sells Orthodox literature and religious paraphernalia. The head of the BOC, Metropolitan Filaret, promised to stop such sales; however, no action has been taken.

In January, the RNE distributed anti-Semitic leaflets in Gomel, which stated: "The Jews are trying to destroy Christianity," "Now hostile activities against the Jews will begin," "The Jews are the forces of evil," and "The fighters against God must be exterminated." In addition, the letters RNE were sprayed on the walls of the Jewish Community building in Gomel. No suspects were arrested.

There were reports of anti-Semitic statements made by public officials. In September 2003, Sergei Kostyan, Deputy Chairman of the International Affairs Committee of the Lower House of Parliament, rejected criticism regarding the installation of a gas pipeline near a Jewish cemetery in Maozyr. Kostyan accused Jews of sowing "ethnic discord." During an October press conference, Information Minister Vladimir Rusakevich said the country should live with Russia like brothers, but to bargain with Russia "like a Yid."

The Committee of Religious and Nationalities Affairs of the Council of Ministers (CRNA) reported that it regularly responded to all public expressions of xenophobia by notifying the government agencies responsible for pursuing legal action against the perpetrators; however, no such legal actions were observed during the period covered by this report.

Belgium

In November, the quasi-governmental Anti-Racism Center (Center for Equal Opportunity and the Struggle against Racism and Other Forms of Discrimination) reported an increase in anti-Semitism in recent years. The Center reported that the annual number of complaints rose to 30 between 2000 and 2003; prior to 1999, an average of 4 anti-Semitic incidents were registered per year. There were 40 complaints filed in the first 11 months of the year. The most serious incident was the stabbing of a Jewish youth in Antwerp. Most complaints concerned anti-Semitism in the media, on the Internet, graffiti, and verbal abuse. An Anti-Racism Center spokesperson pointed out that the increase in the number of incidents is partially due to increased reporting resulting from greater public awareness.

On January 28, during an indoor Belgium-Israel soccer match in the city of Hasselt, spectators with Hamas and Hizballah banners heckled the Israelis and shouted anti-Semitic slogans, some in Arabic. The city of Hasselt, the Anti-Racism Center, and a local Jewish organization filed a criminal complaint over the incident a few days later, which the police continued to pursue actively. No arrests were made during the reporting period. In February, a group of students at a Jewish school in Brussels were assaulted by youths from the neighborhood, which is inhabited primarily by Muslim immigrants.

In late June, there were several incidents of physical attacks on Jewish citizens. These incidents were prominently covered in the national media. On June 24, a number of allegedly North African youths assaulted four Jewish students as they departed their Jewish school in an Antwerp suburb; one fleeing student was stabbed and seriously injured. Jewish students at the school previously had been subjected to verbal insult and harassment from these youths. On June 26, three Jewish students from the same school were harassed by four youths in a car. One fired what is believed to be a toy gun at the students before driving away; there were no injuries. Later that evening, elsewhere in the Antwerp suburbs, a 13-year-old Jewish boy was beaten by three youths. An 11-year-old Moroccan and two Belgians, ages 8 and 16, were arrested and charged with racially motivated assault and battery by a court for youthful offenders; they were required to apologize to the victim and pay damages. Also that evening, several immigrant youths reportedly kicked a Jewish youth repeatedly on the main street of Antwerp, before escaping.

On October 30, at a youth soccer match involving Maccabi Soccer Club, an Antwerp-based team composed mainly of Jewish players, members of the opposite team shouted "Heil Hitler" and other abusive language. The referee reported the incident in writing to the Belgian Soccer Federation. On November 18, the Federation suspended the offending team for a year and fined it $335 (250 euro), a considerable sum for an amateur club. The Anti-Racism Center indicated that prosecution was a possibility.

The Jewish community was increasingly concerned about anti-Semitism. Community representatives expressed concern that criticism of Israel, particularly from the left, was increasingly being transferred to the Jewish community. Senior representatives of the Muslim community have vocally condemned anti-Semitic acts and have participated in events organized by the Jewish community.

There continued to be a few cases of anti-Semitic speech generated from extreme right, neo-Nazi groups. These were pursued by the Anti-Racism Center, which won a conviction in September 2003 against two Holocaust deniers, such denial being illegal in the country; the two were sentenced to a year in prison, a $670 (500 euro) fine, and the costs of the trial.

The politically resurgent far right has not only renounced anti-Semitism, but as part of an effort to appeal for Jewish community votes in Antwerp, became a strong supporter of the Jewish community and of stronger Belgian-Israeli relations.

Anti-Semitic acts or speech are illegal. Several lawsuits were filed by government entities or by the Anti-Racism Center, and there already were a few cases of courts issuing guilty verdicts. The Government so far has had limited success in apprehending and convicting (partly as a result of the very slow place of the judicial processes) perpetrators of anti-Semitic acts. In one example of strong government enforcement responsiveness, the police rapidly deployed a heavily armed unit to a Jewish school in reaction to a possible threat.

The Government investigated web sites containing anti-Semitic language with the intent of filing cases under antiracism legislation.

The Government continued to move forward with its action plan against anti-Semitism, which was approved by the Council of Ministers in July. In response to the anti-Semitic incidents of the past year, protection for the Jewish community and its institutions was strengthened. Ministerial changes over the summer may have slowed implementation, but the commitment remained firm and effort continued.

The Minister of Social Integration convoked a working group that included the Ministers of Justice and Interior, enforcement agencies, the Anti-Racism Center, and representatives of the Jewish community. In May, she also mandated the compilation of research on the problem and perceptions of it. Promotion of tolerance education is a major element of the Government's action plan against anti-Semitism.

Government officials at all levels, including the Prime Minister, promptly condemned anti-Semitic incidents and remained in close touch with the Jewish community. On June 26, the federal Minister of Justice announced that she would require investigating magistrates to prosecute those engaged in anti-Semitic acts, whether verbal, physical, or on the Internet. On June 28, at a demonstration to protest growing anti-Semitism, the mayor of Antwerp promised the city's Jewish community that the police would make the problem their highest priority. On June 29, the federal Minister of Interior announced increased police protection at places such as schools and synagogues and said that the federal government would investigate other measures. On June 30, Prime Minister Verhofstadt met Jewish community leaders, expressed the Government's concern regarding recent attacks, and noted the increased police protection. The following day, he told Parliament that such incidents were attacks on the country's fundamental values and institutions and would not be tolerated. The judicial system has been tasked with giving such attacks full priority. For example, in Brussels, 61 investigations and an indictment were underway, with similar efforts in Antwerp. The Prime Minister also pledged to urge the regions to intensify educational efforts to counter anti-Semitism and racism. Jewish community leaders have indicated to foreign diplomatic observers that they were reassured by government efforts, but they remained apprehensive regarding new outbreaks of violence.

Investigations revealed that some recent attacks on Jews had criminal or personal, not anti-Semitic origins.

Bosnia-Herzegovina

The small Jewish community membership was estimated to be between 500 and 1000 persons. The community maintained a special place in society by virtue of its long history of coexistence with other religious communities, and its active role in mediating among those communities. However, isolated acts of vandalism were reported. For example, in September, several tombstones in the Jewish cemetery in Sarajevo were vandalized. Jewish leaders state that there was a growing tendency in the country to mix anti-Israeli sentiment with acts of anti-Semitism, as the general public and media often fail to distinguish between criticism of Israeli policy and anti-Semitic rhetoric. Following the terrorist attack against a mosque in Turkey during the reporting period, the Jewish community was quickly granted police security at its synagogues and no incidents were reported.

Bulgaria

The Jewish population is estimated to total 3,000 persons. The Bulgarian Helsinki Committee (BHC), in cooperation with Shalom, the primary Jewish organization in the country, conducted a survey of all print media from December 2002 through December 2003 for instances of anti-Semitic and anti-Israeli articles and comments. The project examined 2,162 Jewish/Israeli-related articles and found only around 7 percent to be anti-Semitic, anti-Israeli, or pro-extremist; of these, over 50 percent were anti-Israeli. Of these negative articles, 74 percent were concentrated in two publications (52 percent in Monitor and 22 percent in Sega), which combined make up a small segment of the national mass media; the articles in Sega tended to be exclusively critical of Israel and its policies.

Croatia

The Croatian Jewish community has approximately 2,000 members and had generally good relations with the police and other governmental institutions. In June, a member of the municipal council in Dubrovnik commented on a potential Jewish hotel investor that when, "choosing between Serbs and Jews, Jews were still a greater evil." Local authorities and the Government condemned the comments; the local branch of the ruling party took no disciplinary action against its member.

The Croatia Working Group of the ITF focused on the implementation of Holocaust-related educational programs, dissemination of academic knowledge on the Holocaust, and preservation of the memory of the victims.

Czech Republic

A small, but persistent and fairly well organized, extreme right-wing movement with anti-Semitic views exists in the country.

In August, unknown vandals toppled approximately 80 tombstones at a Jewish cemetery in the eastern town of Hranice. In October, vandals damaged a memorial to victims of the Holocaust for the second time since it was erected in July in the town of Bohumin. According to local Jewish leader, the memorial was covered in brown paint. The memorial was built on the site of a former synagogue, which was destroyed by fire during World War II. In November, a swastika was daubed on a wall of the ancient Altneu Synagogue in Prague, and two youths were arrested in a pub in Sumerk after they shouted "Heil Hitler." They continued giving the Nazi salute even after police removed them from the pub.

In October and November 2003, unknown vandals damaged gravestones at Jewish cemeteries in eastern Bohemia. In November 2003, police in the northern Bohemian town of Krupka apprehended two youths painting Nazi symbols on a monument to the victims of a World War II death march.

On January 30, police arrested Denis Gerasimov, member of the Russian Neo-Nazi band Kolovkrat, and charged him with supporting and propagating a movement aimed at suppressing human rights. Gerasimov was detained at Prague's Ruzyne International Airport after police found large amounts of Nazi propaganda in his luggage. His case was pending at year's end.

The Ministry of Interior continued its efforts to counter the neo-Nazis, which included monitoring their activities, close cooperation with police units in neighboring countries, and concentrated efforts to shut down unauthorized concerts and gatherings of neo-Nazi groups.

Denmark

From January through June, there were five incidents of anti-Semitic vandalism, primarily graffiti, and one incident of an anti-Semitic mailing, which the Government criticized and investigated. Reported incidents also involved theft and racist Internet and written messages. Minority group members were sometimes the perpetrators of the incidents. The Government effectively investigated and dealt with cases of racially motivated violence.

The law prohibits publicly disseminated statements that threaten, insult, or degrade persons based on their religion. In November 2003, the Government launched an action plan to Promote Equal Treatment and Diversity and Combat Racism (Equal Treatment Plan). Although not exclusively aimed at anti-Semitism, the goal of the Equal Treatment Plan was to ensure protection for all citizens, regardless of their beliefs. Under the Equal Treatment Plan, the Government allocated $416,000 (2.5 million DKK) for education and integration programs to combat religious discrimination.

Estonia

During the reporting period, a number of World War II veterans groups held commemorations for Estonians who fought in German uniform (including that of the Waffen SS) against the Soviet occupation. In one case a monument was erected depicting a soldier in Waffen SS uniform, absent Nazi insignia. The Government had the monument removed in September. There were reports that participants made anti-Semitic remarks in response to international criticism of these events.

The commemorations generated considerable public commentary on how Estonia could appropriately honor its war dead. The Government subsequently tasked the Ministry of Population and Ethnic Affairs with creating a plan for an appropriate memorial, and a nonpartisan parliamentary commission has been established for that purpose.

In March, two persons were arrested in the northeastern town of Sillamae for painting anti-Semitic slogans and swastikas on the walls of a building. They were charged with incitement. On April 16, the rabbi of a synagogue in Tallinn found a swastika painted on the building.

In June 2003, three skinheads were sentenced to conditional imprisonment for activities that publicly incited hatred on the basis of national origin and race. They were convicted for having drawn swastikas and anti-Semitic inscriptions on buildings in Sillamae. There are two pending investigations related to the posting of anti-Semitic remarks on the Internet.

The country introduced an annual Holocaust and Other Crimes against Humanity Memorial Day in January 2003. Members of the parliament and ambassadors attended the ceremony marking the first observation of this day in Tallinn.

Following a July meeting with the President of the Jewish Community of Estonia, the Prime Minister said that the Government "was determined to condemn any signs of anti-Semitism and racism." He also said that the Government needed to continue raising awareness of the country's recent history.

At the Berlin OSCE Anti-Semitism Conference in April, the Minister of Population and Ethnic Affairs said that government preparation of law enforcement officers would have to include sensitivity training so the country could more effectively act against manifestations of intolerance, xenophobia, racism and anti-Semitism.

Finland

There were a few reports of anti-Semitic activity, chiefly graffiti such as swastikas with anti-Semitic slogans being spray-painted in public locales. Support for the Palestinians was strong, and critiques of Israeli policy occasionally took on anti-Semitic features. The Helsingin Sanomat, the country's largest newspaper, ran a political cartoon in a magazine supplement that was interpreted by members of the Jewish community and others as anti-Semitic. The newspaper subsequently apologized.

The Government condemned the resurgence of anti-Semitism in Europe. In June, the Justice Ministry ruled that the distributor of an anti-Semitic book was liable under the country's "hate speech" provisions; the distributor was ordered to pay a fine and the book was removed from circulation. The Parliament and a local NGO cosponsored a conference in Helsinki on anti-Semitism, and officials played an active role in international conferences and fora on anti-Semitism. The Government sponsored a visit of a Holocaust survivor to the country to speak with schoolchildren about the Jewish experience during World War II.

France

The Government reports that there were 510 anti-Semitic incidents (both actions and threats) in the first 6 months of the year, as compared to 593 for all of 2003 and 932 for 2002. Interior Minister Dominique de Villepin announced in August that there were 160 attacks against persons or property in the first 7 months of 2004 versus 75 during the same period in 2003. More recently, Justice Minister Dominique Perben stated that there were 298 anti-Semitic acts between January 1 and August 20, of which 162 were attacks against property, 67 were assaults against individuals, and 69 were press violations. This compares, according to Perben, with 108 for all of 2003.

The National Consultative Commission on Human Rights (NCCHR) released an extensive analysis of anti-Semitic incidents reported by the police in 2003. Such incidents ranged from graffiti and desecration (256) and verbal or written harassment (166) to the diffusion of written tracts (31) and bomb threats (10). There were 21 persons injured in anti-Semitic attacks in 2003. Based on investigations of the attacks, the NCCHR stated its conclusions that disaffected French-North African youths were responsible for many of the incidents, which French officials linked to tensions in Israel and the Palestinian territories. A small number of incidents were also attributed to extreme-right and extreme-left organizations.

In its report on anti-Semitic attacks in 2003, the NCCHR focused on an increase in the proportion of anti-Semitic incidents that took place in schools. In 2003, 22 of 125 attacks (18 percent) and 73 of 463 threats (16 percent) occurred in schools; the report shows this to be the highest proportion of incidents in schools since 1997, the oldest data in the report.

On May 30, in Boulogne-Billancourt, a 17-year-old Jewish youth was attacked outside his home by a group of young men yelling anti-Semitic slogans. The youth is the son of a local rabbi.

In June, an individual shouting "Allah Akbar" stabbed a Jewish student and assaulted two other Jewish students in the city of Epinay-sur-Seine. This same person is believed to be responsible for similar knife attacks on five other victims, including those of Haitian and Algerian origin. A suspect, reportedly identified by several of the victims, was in custody at the end of the period covered by this report. The varied and random nature of the victims made the true motive of the attacks hard to discern.

In 2003, some Jewish groups were outraged when a court ordered that--in the case of two 11-year-old Muslim youths expelled for accusations of physical and verbal attacks against a Jewish student--the two students be readmitted to school, and also ordered the Government to reimburse the families $1,340 (1,000 euro) each for court costs. The courts found that, while the behavior of the Muslim students merited action, the age of the students and the circumstances did not justify expulsion.

On March 23, in Toulon, a Jewish synagogue and community center was set on fire. According to media reports, the arsonist broke a window and threw a Molotov cocktail into the building. There was minor damage and no injuries.

On May 7, in Villier-le-Bel, a small explosive device was discovered outside a synagogue north of Paris. According to media reports, the bomb was in a bag with the writing "Boom anti-Jews" and a swastika. On May 14, an 18-year-old man was found guilty of putting the fake bombs on the grounds of the synagogue and was sentenced to 2 months in prison.

On October 29-30, close to 100 gravestones were desecrated at a Jewish cemetery in Brumath, just outside Strasbourg. The vandals painted swastikas and "SS" symbols on 92 Jewish gravestones.

In November 2003, Hizballah's Al-Manar satellite television channel broadcast an anti-Semitic, Egyptian pseudo-documentary called "Ash

Shatat" (The Diaspora). The Government and Jewish organizations strongly criticized Al-Manar for the blatant anti-Semitism of this series and for the incendiary intent of some of Al-Manar's news coverage. These complaints against Al-Manar prompted the Audio Visual Superior Council (CSA) to seek to cut off Al-Manar's dissemination via its France-based satellite operator, Eutelsat. France's highest appeals court for regulatory matters, the Conseil d'Etat, ruled in August that Al-Manar could continue satellite broadcasting pending application for a broadcast license from the CSA. The CSA then entered into negotiations with Al-Manar that resulted in the agreement and temporary license. The CSA signed a 1-year, limited license with Al-Manar on November 19 that included provisions banning anti-Semitic broadcasts, propaganda in favor of suicide bombings, and the diffusion of hate. The CSA's reversal of its decision to cut off Al-Manar was vigorously protested by Jewish organizations. Shortly thereafter, the CSA petitioned the Conseil d'Etat to ban the station based on anti-Semitic programming broadcast after Al-Manar signed the restricted license. On December 13, the Conseil d'Etat ordered Eutelsat to cease broadcasts of Al-Manar within 48 hours. Prime Minister Raffarin has called Al-Manar's anti-Semitic programming "incompatible with French values" and urged the issue of satellite broadcasts be taken up at the EU level. Authorities are similarly investigating Iranian-broadcast Al-Alam channel.

Government officials at the highest level vigorously and publicly condemned acts of anti-Semitism. In October, the Ministry of Foreign Affairs called comments by Radio France International editor Alain Menargues "unacceptable." In an interview publicizing his book on the West Bank security barrier, Menargues called Israel a "racist" state. Menargues was forced to resign as a result of his comments.

Of these anti-Semitic acts committed during the reporting period, the Minister of Justice reported that suspects have been identified in 59 of the cases, resulting in 46 cases going to court and 13 cases closed after the offender paid a fine or was found legally inculpable. Of the 2003 incidents, the Government reported that police had sufficient evidence to question 91 suspects, arrest 69 suspects, and bring to trial 43 suspects. In 2003, there were 7 convictions for anti-Semitic attacks committed that year and 15 convictions for attacks committed in 2002; punishments ranged from fines to 4 years' imprisonment.

Authorities condemned anti-Semitic attacks, maintained heightened security at Jewish institutions, investigated the attacks, made arrests, and pursued prosecutions. More than 13 mobile units, totaling more than 1,200 police officers, were assigned to those locales having the largest Jewish communities. Fixed or mobile police were present in the schools, particularly during the hours when children are entering or leaving school buildings. All of these measures were coordinated closely with leaders of the Jewish communities in the country, notably the Representative Council of Jewish Institutions in France (CRIF). In addition, the Ministry of Interior has earmarked $20.1 million (15 million euro) for additional security at Jewish sites.

In November 2003, after an arson attack destroyed a Jewish school in Gagny, President Chirac stated, "An attack on a Jew is an attack on France" and ordered the formation of an interministerial committee charged with leading an effort to combat anti-Semitism. Since its first meeting in December 2003, the committee has worked to improve government coordination in the fight against anti-Semitism, including the timely publication of statistics and reinforced efforts to prosecute attackers.

In June, the Government commissioned Jean-Cristophe Rufin, a doctor, writer, and president of the humanitarian association Action Against Hunger, to prepare an in-depth report on racism and anti-Semitism in the country. The Rufin Report, released in October, concluded that racism and anti-Semitism attacked the country's republican values and threatened democracy. The report identified the perpetrators of anti-Semitic acts as elements of the extreme right, Maghrebian (North African origin) youth, and "disaffected individuals" whose anti-Semitic obsessions prompt their attacks against Jews and Jewish institutions. The Rufin Report also warned against radical anti-Zionists who question Israel's right to exist. The report recommended that a law be created to punish those publicly equating Israel or Zionism with apartheid or Nazism. The report also recommended removing injunctions against incitement to racism and anti-Semitism from the press law and writing a new law, specific to those crimes. The current provisions in the press law are too cumbersome for prosecuting public hate speech and too lenient in their sanctions against private hate speech, it notes.

Many local and international Jewish organizations, as well as foreign governments, praised the Government for vigorous action in combating anti-Semitism; however, some groups asserted that the judicial system was lax in its sentencing of anti-Semitic offenders.

The Government took steps to combat intolerance, particularly among the youth. In March, the Government published an educational tool, intended to help public school teachers promote tolerance and combat anti-Semitism and racism; however, it is still too early to judge its efficacy. In August, Paris Mayor Bertrand Delanoe sent letters to all Paris-area school principals calling for "debates on anti-Semitism, racism and discrimination" when classes resume in September. In addition, the Minister of Education called for a national debate in schools at the beginning of the academic year to highlight the need for tolerance and announced that 5,500 schools would receive copies of the film "Shoah" for use in classroom education. These actions followed the creation of a National Commission to Combat anti-Semitism in schools in 2003.

The Government has taken other proactive steps to fight anti-Semitic attacks, including instructing police commissioners to create monitoring units in each department and announcing in June the creation of a department-level Council of Religions that will raise public awareness of increased racial and anti-sectarian incidents. In September, the Mayor of Paris launched a campaign to fight all forms of intolerance that included 1,200 municipal billboards and bulletins in major newspapers.

Germany

Approximately 87,500 persons are members of Jewish congregations and account for 0.1 percent of the population. According to press reports, the country's Jewish population is growing rapidly; more than 100,000 Jews from the former Soviet Union have come to the country since 1990, with smaller numbers arriving from other countries as well. Not all new arrivals join congregations, resulting in the discrepancy between population numbers and the number of congregation members.

While anti-Semitism based on religious doctrines and traditional anti-Jewish prejudices continued to exist, Jewish leaders, academics, and others believe that a newer, nontraditional form of anti-Semitism is emerging in the country. This form tends to promote anti-Semitism as part of its other stands against globalization, capitalism, Zionism, and foreigners. According to the 2003 report by the Office for the Protection of the Constitution, the total number of registered anti-Semitic crimes decreased to 1,199 (from 1,515 in 2002). However, among these, the number of violent crimes increased from 28 to 35, and the number of desecrations of Jewish cemeteries, synagogues, or memorials went up from 78 to 115.

On July 22, a 15-year-old boy in Hagen, along with two others, threatened synagogue visitors with a knife and made anti-Semitic remarks.

On July 31, a young man wearing a Star of David sticker was walking on a street in Pankow, a suburb of Berlin, when a right-wing extremist put a National Democratic Party (NPD) leaflet in his hand. After dropping the leaflet on the sidewalk, the rightist attempted to strangle the victim and throw him on the ground. The victim had minor injuries, and the police arrested the offender.

In August, the Zionist Organization of Frankfurt received an eyewitness report that four men harassed an English-speaking orthodox Jew in downtown Frankfurt. According to the report, the men shouted "they forgot to send your parents to the gas chamber" and jostled the individual until he fell to the ground. The men fled the scene immediately. Police refused to disclose the victim's identity or other information on the incident.

An ancient Jewish cemetery in Duesseldorf was desecrated in June. Forty-five gravestones were covered with swastikas, SS signs, and anti-Jewish slogans. Other Jewish cemeteries, including in Bochum, Nickenich, and Bausendorf, were vandalized during the reporting period. Police investigators were unable to identify the perpetrators.

On September 23, 350 people demonstrated in the district of Neunkirchen (Saarland) against the desecration of the Hermanstrasse Jewish cemetery earlier in the month. According to police, the desecration nearly destroyed the cemetery. Vandals have desecrated the Hermanstrasse graves on 10 occasions since 1971, including twice during the reporting period. The incident took place after significant electoral gains by the far-right party NPD in Neunkirchen (5.6 percent) and neighboring Voelklingen (9.7 percent) in Saarland's September 5 state elections.

During the reporting period, the extreme right wing "National Democratic Party" (NPD) organized two demonstrations in the city of Bochum under the motto "stop the construction of the synagogue - give the 4 million to the people!"

Jewish community leaders expressed disappointment in the leaders of other religious communities, as well as in some local and national politicians, for not speaking out more forcefully against anti-Semitism. In October 2003, Martin Hohmann, a Christian Democratic Union (CDU) Member of Parliament, publicly compared the actions of Jews during the Russian Revolution to those of the Nazis during the Holocaust. These remarks led to a criminal complaint alleging incitement and slander and to the opening of an inquiry. Hohmann was expelled from the CDU Bundestag Caucus in November 2003 and from the CDU Hesse state organization in July. Leading politicians from all major parties continued to assert that neo-Nazi groups posed a serious threat to public order and to call for continuing vigilance by law enforcement agencies. On the other hand, some observers blamed the actions in the Middle East for rising anti-Semitism.

Frankfurt's Jewish community harshly criticized anti-Semitism on the part of some Islamic representatives at the October Frankfurt Book Fair. Jewish representatives cited open displays of anti-Semitic texts such as the Saudi Arabian book "Terror and Zionist Thinking" (featuring a cover illustration of a person standing in a pool of blood with a skull and a Star of David).

The Aachen-based Islamist group, the Al Aqsa Association, which was banned by Federal Interior Minister Otto Schilly in 2002 due to its financial support of the terrorist organization Hamas, lodged an appeal against the ban at the Federal Administrative Court in August 2002. In July, the court decided to suspend the ban until conclusion of the proceedings. In a final decision on December 3, the Federal Administrative Court in Leipzig confirmed the ban of the Al Aqsa Association.

Nine members of the Kameradschaft Sd, a neo-Nazi gang from Southern Germany, were charged in an alleged 2003 plot to bomb the site of a planned Jewish community center in downtown Munich. The first of two trials started in October involving three teenage girls and two men. The public has been largely excluded from this trial in order to protect the defendant minors. The trial of the alleged ringleader, Martin Wiese, and three members of his inner leadership circle began in November.

Distribution of the propaganda of proscribed organizations, statements inciting racial hatred and endorsing Nazism, and denial of the Holocaust are illegal, and the authorities sought to block what they considered dangerous material on the Internet. In March, police nationwide raided over 300 apartments to search for and seize right-wing extremist CDs and other banned music products. The state of Lower Saxony took legal action against some of the growing number of neo-Nazi musical bands in the state, which called for violence or employed xenophobic or racist lyrics. In 2003, members of the Berlin neo-Nazi band "Landser" were convicted of forming a criminal organization and sentenced to terms ranging from 21 months probation to 3 years and 4 months in prison.

Officials estimated that there were more than 1,000 Internet sites with what they considered to be objectionable or dangerous right-wing extremist content. The Federal Court of Justice held that the country's laws against Nazi incitement might apply to individuals who post Nazi material on Internet sites available to users in the country, even if the site resides on a foreign server.

In April, the Government hosted a historic Organization for Security and Cooperation in Europe (OSCE) conference on anti-Semitism. With strong support from the Government, the conference led to a declaration calling on OSCE member states to implement a set of concrete measures to combat anti-Semitism.

Authorities ran a variety of tolerance-education programs, many focusing on anti-Semitism and xenophobia. Government agencies cooperated with NGOs in the formulation and administration of these programs. These measures included promoting educational programs that not only fight anti-Semitism, but also remember the Holocaust and foster tolerance and respect for all religious groups; collecting and maintaining information of anti-Semitic incidents and other hate crimes; and compiling best practices. With active participation from the Muslim community, Hamburg has begun work on establishing interreligious education at public schools, labeled the "Hamburg Model."

Greece

Vandalism of Jewish monuments continued to be a problem during the reporting period; however, the Government condemned the acts. Jewish monuments in Ioannina were desecrated three times in 2003. The Holocaust memorial in Thessaloniki was desecrated in February 2003. Police have not found perpetrators. Anti-Semitic graffiti was painted, removed by authorities, and repainted in several places on the busy Athens-Corinth Highway. The extreme right-wing group "Golden Dawn" regularly paints anti-Semitic graffiti on bridges and other structures throughout Greece. Some schoolbooks still carry negative references to Roman Catholics, Jewish persons, and others. Bookstores in Northern Greece sold and displayed anti-Semitic literature including "The Protocols of the Elders of Zion."

The Wiesenthal Center issued a travel advisory in November 2003 warning Jewish visitors about "the failure of Greece to curb growing anti-Semitism;" however, local Jewish community leaders do not support the advisory. The National Tourist Organization continued to promote on its website Easter traditions such as the burning of an effigy of Judas on some islands, sometimes known locally as the "burning of the Jew," which propagate hatred and fanaticism against Jews. The Wiesenthal Center protested the revival of this tradition.

Anti-Semitism continued to exist, both in the mainstream and extremist press. The Wiesenthal Center and the ADL denounced the press for anti-Semitic articles and cartoons on several occasions, particularly after Israeli forces killed Hamas leader Sheik Yassin. The line between opposition to Israeli policies and attitudes toward Jews in general is often blurred, giving rise to anti-Semitic sentiment in the media and among the public.

The mainstream media often use the terms "genocide" and "Holocaust" to describe the situation in Israel and the West Bank/Gaza, drawing a parallel with Nazi Germany. The press and public often do not clearly distinguish between Israeli policies and Jews. The Jewish community leaders have condemned anti-Semitic broadcasts on small private television stations, but no charges have been brought against these largely unlicensed operators.

The renowned composer Mikis Theodorakis called Jews "the root of evil" in November 2003, and made strong anti-Semitic remarks during the reporting period. Government officials stated that Theodorakis' statements were directed against Israel and not against the Jewish people.

Populist Orthodox Rally (LAOS), a small, extreme right-wing party, supports virulent nationalism, anti-Semitism, racism, and xenophobia. LAOS's leader, George Karatzaferis, won a seat in the European Parliament in June elections. Karatzaferis regularly attributes negative events involving Greece to international Jewish plots. He used the party-owned television station to denounce politicians with Jewish origins and to claim that Jews were behind the September 11 attacks.

The Government condemned all acts of vandalism. The Government provided 24-hour police protection to Jewish Community offices in Athens and other major cities. Negotiations between the Jewish Community of Thessaloniki and the Government to find acceptable recompense for the community's cemetery were ongoing.

The Constitution establishes the Eastern Orthodox Church of Christ (Greek Orthodoxy) as the prevailing religion, but also provides for the rights of all citizens to practice the religion of their choice. Jews freely practice their religion, and Jewish organizations have not complained or requested additional legal protection.

Judaism is one of the three religious groups (the others are Greek Orthodox and Islam) considered to be "legal persons of public law." In practice, this beneficial distinction primarily means that Jewish organizations can own property as religious entities rather than as legal entities.

On January 15, the Parliament unanimously approved the declaration of January 27, the day Auschwitz was liberated, as Holocaust Remembrance Day. The following week, the country commemorated Holocaust Remembrance Day with events in Athens and Thessaloniki and the participation of Nobel Laureate Elie Wiesel. In April, a commemorative stone was placed at the railway station from which Jews were deported to concentration camps.

In October, the Government participated in the organization of a seminar on "Teaching the Holocaust." Held under the auspices of the Ministry of Education, it addressed 150 educators and Athens University education majors. This teacher-training seminar aimed to introduce Holocaust education in primary and secondary schools.

A memorial to Greek-Jewish veterans of World War II was unveiled in October 2003 in Thessaloniki.

Hungary

The Jewish community stated that there were fewer acts of vandalism in Jewish cemeteries than in 2003, attributed most of the incidents to youths, and did not consider the incidents anti-Semitic.

On July 1, a Jewish cemetery in northern Hungary was vandalized. More than 90 gravestones were smashed just weeks after the local town council had renovated the cemetery to mark the 60th anniversary of the Holocaust.

Representatives of the Jewish community expressed concern over anti-Semitism in some media outlets, in society, and in coded political speech. For example, certain segments of an ongoing Sunday news magazine, Vasarnapi Ujsag, on Hungarian Public Radio were criticized for presenting guests who held anti-Semitic viewpoints. In October 2003, a weekly talk show, Ejjeli Menedek, reported on Holocaust denier David Irving, who made derogatory statements regarding Jewish persons. The show was subsequently cancelled. The weekly newspaper Magyar Demokrata published anti-Semitic articles and featured articles by authors who have denied the Holocaust.

Jewish Community Mazsihisz representatives requested the Ministry of Cultural Heritage to close a county museum exhibition highlighting the Arrow Cross and Hungarian nationalism during World War II. The exhibition was closed, and the materials were returned to their owners. During their visit to the country in April, the Chief Rabbi and the President of Israel spoke positively of the situation of the Jewish community in Hungary.

Local NGOs are attempting to get a court order stripping the neo-Nazi group "Blood and Honor" of its official registration. A new unregistered neo-Nazi group, "Hungarian Future," planned a public demonstration to commemorate the 60th anniversary of the fascist takeover of the country. Several groups have planned anti-fascist counter demonstrations for the same day and at the same locale. The police have found no legal grounds on which to ban the demonstration.

On April 5, hundreds of persons participated in the unveiling ceremony of a statue of Pal Teleki, the Prime Minister of Hungary in the 1920s, who was the first in Europe to enact anti-Semitic legislation. The Minister of Culture, Istvan Hiller, cancelled plans for setting up the statue (in Budapest) in the wake of pressures from the Wiesenthal Center. The statue, which was to have been set up opposite the President's official residence in Budapest, was eventually built in the courtyard opposite the Catholic church in the town of Balatonbolgar on the shore of Lake Balaton.

The Government made strong efforts to combat anti-Semitism by clearly speaking out against the use of coded speech by right-wing extremists, and the Prime Minister himself publicly stated that Hungarians were also responsible for the Holocaust.

The 1997 changes to the hate speech law that were intended to resolve conflicting court decisions and make it easier to enforce and stiffen penalties for hate crimes committed on the basis of the victim's ethnicity, race, or nationality proved inadequate and often led to conflicting court decisions. In early 2003, the Office of the Prosecutor successfully prosecuted a member of the extremist Justice and Life Party for publishing an anti-Semitic article in a local newspaper. In November 2003, the Budapest Appeals Court acquitted a former Member of Parliament, who is a Calvinist pastor, of a charge of incitement to hatred. The conflicting court decisions prompted Parliament to pass a more restrictive law on hate speech, this time incorporating religious groups within its scope. Pressured from both the right and the left, President Madl referred it to the Constitutional Court for an advisory opinion in January. In May, the Constitutional Court ruled that the law is too vague and returned it to Parliament for refinement.

Iceland

Harassment of the Jewish community in the country was infrequent and not organized. The absence of anti-Semitism may have been due to the fact that the Jewish population was tiny and inconspicuous. Iceland had no synagogue, no Jewish community center, and no Jewish religious services available. The Jewish population had yet to organize formally and register as a religious community under applicable law. Anti-Semitism rarely figured in Icelandic news reports. The Government and NGOs had no programs to counter anti-Semitism.

One incident of harassment was reported in August. A Jewish visitor reported in an online news magazine that he and a friend had been harassed by a group of young teenagers who pointed at his yarmulke, gave a 'Heil Hitler' salute, and then briefly blocked the visitors' exit from a parking lot, intimidating them. An Icelandic daily newspaper picked up the story, sparking over 30 online comments from Iceland-based correspondents. Some of the comments were themselves anti-Semitic or xenophobic in tone and content.

The March 22 issue of Icelandic tabloid newspaper DV carried a cartoon that raised concerns in the small Jewish community. The drawing showed a flying saucer that had touched down next to Jerusalem's Western Wall. Two smiling aliens, anthropomorphized as swastikas, were disembarking and pointing. Their speech balloon contained nonsense signs. Facing them and bearing expressions of shock were two Orthodox Jews, with hats, tallis, black coats, and sidelocks. The cartoon's caption stated, "The 'Galactic Council' regarded the situation in the Middle East on the planet Earth as threatening to the stability of the solar system, viewed in the long term, and thus sent its best negotiators, Zorg and Xuri, to the scene for talks." The cartoonist seemed to be suggesting that the solution to the Middle East conflict would be to dispatch Nazis to Israel's capital.

Holocaust education was not required by the national curriculum. However, the Ministry of Education mandated that the subject be covered as part of mandatory history education. References to the Holocaust appeared in several textbooks that touch on Nazism and persecution against Jews and other minorities in 1930s and 1940s Germany and in the countries it occupied. According to staff of the state textbook producer, teachers were permitted to take the initiative for more in-depth teaching on the subject than the little that was offered in textbooks.

Ireland

During the reporting period, the Irish Times newspaper reported three instances of anti-Semitism in the country. One incident included a swastika painted on the Irish Jewish Museum in Dublin, while the other incidents involved vandalism at a Jewish cemetery and synagogue. A 2003 study by the European Commission's European Monitoring Center on Racism and Xenophobia described the country as having "relatively little reported in the way of a problem with anti-Semitism." In fact, the study categorized all the 2003 cases as "abusive behavior" (threatening letters or phone calls), totaling only 16. Recent evidence shows that these acts may be interrelated with the emergence of a racist group calling itself Irish Nationalist, which has expressed anti-British and anti-Israeli views. In spite of these developments, the country has very little evidence of anti-Semitism.

The most recent study, published by the Government's National Consultative Committee on Racism and Interculturalism (NCCRI), showed increases in "cases of abuse or discrimination, which is above average from past studies." However, further research of most of these cases occurred soon after a citizenship referendum was held in May, that allowed citizens to vote on whether or not being born in Ireland provided automatic citizenship. It was discovered that most of the reported abuse and discrimination cases involved refugees and new immigrants. In spite of this slight increase, only one percent of discrimination reports were based on racial or ethnic origin. In addition, the Irish Police's (An Garda Siochana) Racial and Intercultural Unit also "records racially motivated crime" and provides police with instruction booklets on how to interact with different ethnic, cultural, and racial groups. The Police Commissioner has also appointed Police Ethnic Liaison Officers in district and divisional police stations throughout the country. The country consistently follows the EU laws and regulations regarding religious tolerance.

During its EU Presidency, Ireland encouraged all member states to be pro-active in combating anti-Semitism and explained how proper education and training about anti-Semitism, human rights, and cultural diversity would strengthen the EU community and reduce discrimination. On the international level, the country has sponsored a UN Resolution on Religious Tolerance for the last 20 years. In response to Israel's request that anti-Semitism be specifically mentioned in the annual resolution for 2003, Ireland proposed a General Assembly resolution on anti-Semitism, which all EU member states supported.

Italy

Surveys conducted by independent research centers confirmed the persistence of some societal prejudices against Judaism. Recent public opinion surveys indicate that anti-Semitism is growing in Italy. According to pollsters, this trend is tied to, and in some cases fed by, widespread opposition to the Sharon Government and popular support for the Palestinian cause. There have been examples of anti-Semitic graffiti in several large cities. In November, vandals desecrated several graves at a Jewish cemetery in Reggio Emilia, but no anti-Semitic signs or inscriptions were found at the site.

In January, Prime Minister Berlusconi created a new "Inter-Ministerial Commission to Combat Anti-Semitism" to ensure strong, uniform responses to any anti-Semitic acts by the police and government officials. In April, the mayor of Rome announced the establishment of a museum dedicated to the Shoah. In November, the Government created a new office to combat racial and ethnic discrimination through education, mass media campaigns, and judicial assistance to victims of discrimination. The new office lists Muslims, Jews, and foreign workers as the three cultural minorities most likely to face racial or ethnic prejudice in the country. In 2003, the Parliament approved the creation of a National Holocaust Memorial Museum in Ferrara; planning is in process, but construction has not begun. In November 2003, newly appointed Foreign Minister (and Deputy Prime Minister) Gianfranco Fini publicly repudiated his party's Fascist origins, condemned Mussolini's treatment of the Jews, and sought forgiveness during a historic visit to Israel.

The Government hosted meetings to increase educational awareness of the Holocaust and to combat anti-Semitism in Europe.

The country commemorated Holocaust Remembrance Day on January 27. During the reporting period, thousands marched in commemorative processions across the country, several cities staged exhibitions of the 'memory train' used to transport Italian Jews to Nazi concentration camps, and Italian public school students participated in educational and commemorative programs in schools.

With the Foreign Ministry and the Office of the Prime Minister, the Anti-Defamation League hosted a conference on anti-Semitism in Rome in December. Prime Minister Berlusconi, Foreign Minister Fini, and other high-ranking Italian officials participated in the conference.

The Vatican made a serious effort to combat anti-Semitism. The Holy See is active in OSCE endeavors and sent a high-level delegation to the April OSCE anti-Semitism conference in Berlin. A Vatican document released on March 8, instructed bishops on the exercise of their ministry, and implored them to encourage respect for Jews to combat anti-Semitism. It also asked bishops to ensure that the study of Judaism is on the curriculum in their seminaries for priests and to promote dialogue regarding Judaism. The Pope made several statements condemning anti-Semitism. These attracted notice of the Jewish community. For example, Israel's Chief Rabbis expressed thanks to the Pope for his strong condemnation of anti-Semitism during a January 16 audience.

Kazakhstan

Other than the actions of members of Hizb ut-Tahrir, who printed and distributed leaflets that supported anti-Semitism among other beliefs, there were no reports of anti-Semitic incitement or acts during the reporting period. There were reports of anti-Semitic propaganda in pamphlets distributed by followers of Hizb ut-Tahrir. The Government considers Hizb ut-Tahrir to be an illegal extremist group and has taken action to prosecute members engaged in handing out these pamphlets under Articles 164 ("Fanning Social, National, Tribal, Racial or Religious Enmity") and 337 ("Creating An Illicit Public Association and Participating in its activities") of the Criminal Code.

In August, the Chief Rabbi of the country addressed an international religious conference in Brussels, stating that in his 10 years living in Kazakhstan, he had never faced a single case of anti-Semitism, and he praised the Government for its proactive protection of the Jewish community. In July, a visiting rabbi praised the Government for its efforts to promote religious tolerance and dialogue among Christians, Jews, and Muslims. On September 7, the Chief Rabbi of Israel arrived in Astana to attend the opening and dedication of the largest synagogue in Central Asia.

Latvia

There were several incidents of desecration of cemeteries, vandalism, and anti-Semitic graffiti. In September 2003, vandals overturned dozens of tombstones and sprayed anti-Semitic graffiti on the walls of Riga's New Jewish Cemetery. Government leaders moved quickly to denounce the vandalism, and Riga city services cleaned and restored the cemetery within 2 days of the event. Latvian police arrested five youthful suspects the following week, and the Prosecutor General's office indicted them in October 2003. The vandals could face up to 8 years in prison.

In October, a nationalist organization distributed a commemorative envelope bearing the likeness of an aviation pioneer who also participated in the Holocaust. The Foreign Minister condemned the activity.

The Latvian National Front (LNF) is an organization that purports to represent Latvian cultural values. Its director, Aivars Garda, owns and operates a publishing house that publishes nationalist historical texts and a sensationalist newspaper and newsletter called "Deoccupation, Decolonization, Debolshevization" (DDD). The Chief of the Latvian Security Police has stated that the LNF "borders" on being an extremist organization, and the Ministry of Social Integration has asked the Prosecutor General's Office to evaluate whether or not DDD promotes ethnic hatred. A prominent Jewish businessman alleged this year that the website published a call to kill four Latvian Jews.

In 2002, the Government created a new ministry, the Ministry of Social Integration, whose mission is to promote inter-ethnic tolerance by strengthening civil society and encouraging NGOs to create and participate in educational programs that bridge ethnic group boundaries. The ministry was an active voice in political affairs and was a vocal critic of organizations, like the LNF, that perpetrated anti-Semitic sentiments. The Ministry, in November, asked the Prosecutor General's Office to review whether or not the LNF's newsletter "DDD" promotes ethnic hatred and violates state law.

In October 2002, the country became the first Baltic state to sign "The Protection and Preservation of Certain Cultural Properties" agreement that protects and maintains Holocaust sites. The Government is collaborating with the family of noted American-Latvian Jewish painter Mark Rothko to renovate a synagogue in the city of Daugavpils, the town of his birth.

The country has taken many positive steps toward promoting anti-bias and tolerance education. The Government worked on a Holocaust curriculum development project that will change Holocaust education in classrooms, folding the history of the Holocaust into the country's educational materials. In addition, Ministry of Education regulations required teaching about the Holocaust in schools. For the past 5 years, high school teachers participated in Holocaust teaching methodology seminars.

Lithuania

In April, the police launched an investigation into the desecration of a Jewish cemetery in the Kaisiadorys region. They had detained no perpetrators at the end of the period covered by this report.

The country's Jewish communities expressed concern over an increase in anti-Semitic remarks made by extremists and a few mainstream politicians. The political leadership of the country and the national press generally condemned anti-Semitic statements when they occurred.

In April 2003, the Council of Europe (COE) criticized the Government for not taking action against the anti-Semitic statements of individuals seeking political office; the publication of anti-Semitic articles in the media; the distribution of anti-Semitic proclamations and other materials; acts of vandalism against Jewish graves and monuments; and anti-Semitic statements during public gatherings. There were similar occurrences this year; in addition, multiple anonymous anti-Semitic comments appeared on the Internet.

In February, state institutions received anonymous anti-Semitic proclamations. The proclamations railed against Jews, calling them among other things "vampires of the population," an epithet that the country's Ambassador to Israel, Alfonsas Eidintas, cited in his book "Jews, Lithuanians, and the Holocaust" as an example of Nazi propaganda. In response, government representatives publicly condemned anti-Semitism. Also in February, a popular national daily Respublika carried a series of editorials with obvious anti-Semitic undertones. The series was entitled "Who Rules the World?" and the final editorial answered—"the Jews." A cartoon accompanying the series was reminiscent of Nazi propaganda, and featured grotesque caricatures of a Jew and a homosexual supporting a large globe. The editorial blamed Jewish organized crime figures for exploiting the Holocaust tragedy to avoid punishment for their own criminal activities, and it focused on the alleged failure of the Jewish Community to disassociate themselves from such criminals. The main thrust of the article was that Jews are the wealthiest and most powerful societal group in the world and control world events. Government officials at the highest levels condemned the publication of the series and the anti-Semitic sentiments therein, but the Jewish community and others criticized the Government for responding too slowly. Local NGOs and representatives of other religious groups similarly denounced the anti-Semitic articles. The Prosecutor General's Office and the State Security Department launched pre-trial investigations of Respublika's editor-in-chief for inciting ethnic and racial hatred. The case was pending at year's end. In April, the Parliament formed a working group to draft legislation increasing the penalties for inciting discord, anti-Semitism, racism, and xenophobia.

In June 2003, media reports prompted the State Security Department to investigate the publication of "The Protocols of the Elders of Zion" in a low-circulation periodical Zemaitijos Parlamentas, and the publication was discontinued. In December 2003, members of the National Democratic Party, led by a member of the Siauliai city council, attempted to prevent the lighting of a menorah during a Hanukkah celebration and insulted members of the local Jewish community. The Siauliai mayor publicly apologized for the incident.

The Jewish community has argued that, while most school textbooks accurately and fairly present the Holocaust, some perpetuate unfavorable stereotypes of Lithuania's pre-World War II Jewish community and thereby promote intolerance. Although the Ministry of Education attempted to ensure the historical accuracy of school textbooks, the educational system allowed a great deal of leeway for individual teachers to choose their own texts. Teachers are therefore able to use textbooks that are not recommended by the Government and that may portray an unfavorable and outdated view of the country's pre-War Jewish community.

An estimated 10 percent of the population of the country before World War II was Jewish. More than 200,000 Jewish persons (approximately 95 percent of that population) were killed in the Holocaust. The country still was reconciling itself with its past and working to understand it better. In 1998, President Valdas Adamkus established a historical commission to investigate both the crimes of the Holocaust and the subsequent Soviet occupation. The commission has held annual conferences and several seminars, published several reports, and cosponsored a Holocaust education program.

From January to September, the Prosecutor General's Office initiated six investigations of genocide cases, war crimes, and crimes against humanity. These new cases (which brought the total of such cases initiated since 1990 to approximately 188) included six investigations of killings in 1941, according to the Simon Wiesenthal Center. There were 25 such cases, involving 140 to150 individuals, pending in September. The Government continued to support the International Commission to Investigate the Crimes of Nazi and Soviet Occupation Regimes in Lithuania. The Commission, which includes historians, human rights representatives, representatives of international Jewish organizations, and both Lithuanian and foreign lawyers, produced new reports during the reporting period. The Commission in cooperation with Yad Vashem (the Holocaust Martyrs' and Heroes' Remembrance Authority) and other organizations continued to implement a program of Holocaust education, including tolerance development, in the country's schools. The Commission organized conferences and seminars to promote the development of a tolerant civil society.

A March poll indicated that anti-Semitism was more alarming to residents in large cities, while people living in rural areas tended not to notice it. Respondents of older generations had a poorer opinion of Lithuanian-Jewish relations than people aged between 18 and 25 who more often defined relations as good.

The Seimas (Parliament) commemorated Holocaust Day by publicly acknowledging and apologizing for the killing of Jews and destruction of Jewish culture in the country during World War II.

The Government and City of Vilnius continued a program using private funds to rebuild parts of the Jewish quarter in Vilnius with the understanding that the Jewish community will have use of some of the space upon completion of the project. In September 2003, the Government returned 46 Torah scrolls (in addition to 309 such scrolls turned over in January 2002) to an Israeli spiritual and heritage group for distribution among Jewish congregations worldwide.

Macedonia

On March 4, several spectators hung banners with swastikas at a handball match near the city of Bitola. Police officials present did not confront the individuals responsible for the banners, and pictures of the policemen standing in front of the banners appeared in newspapers the following day. Several newspapers published editorials critical of the police's inaction, and the Ministry of the Interior later disciplined the officers in question.

Moldova

In March more than 70 tombstones were desecrated in the Jewish cemetery in Tiraspol, the principal city of the breakaway Transnistria region that is not controlled by the Moldovan authorities. Swastikas and other Nazi symbols were painted on monuments, and many tombstones were damaged beyond repair. On May 4, unknown persons attempted to set the Tiraspol synagogue on fire by throwing a Molotov cocktail onto the premises. The attack failed when passers-by extinguished the fire. Transnistrian authorities believed the attacks were perpetrated by the same persons and claimed they were investigating the incidents.

In February 2003, unknown persons destroyed eight tombstones in a Jewish cemetery in Balti. However, according to a leading rabbi in Chisinau, it was not clear whether anti-Semitism motivated the event.

Netherlands

The National Expertise Center for Discrimination, founded in 1998, deals with cases of discrimination that come under Dutch criminal law and registers all criminal cases in this area. In the years 2000, 2001, 2002 and 2003, the joint prosecutor offices recorded 214, 198, 242 and 204 discrimination cases respectively, of which about a quarter concerned cases of anti-Semitism.

Anti-Semitism, particularly among Muslims, was linked in many cases to the ongoing conflict between Israel and the Palestinians. Most anti-Semitic incidents were not violent and included abusive language, hate mail, verbal insults at soccer matches, Internet "chat room" discussions, as well as persistent historical revisionism (such as Holocaust denial). However, pockets of militant young Muslims, mostly Moroccans, on a number of occasions assaulted or intimidated identifiable Jews. In addition to the anti-Semitic acts carried out by a relatively small group of Arab youths, the virulent anti-Israel sentiment among certain groups in society, such as the Arab European League and the Stop the Occupation movement, also have contributed to an anti-Semitic atmosphere in some quarters.

The Center for Information and Documentation on Israel (CIDI) in its latest report covering the period January 2003 to May 2004 registered 334 anti-Semitic incidents in 2003, compared to 359 in 2002, the first decrease (7.5 percent) in anti-Semitic incidents since 2000. In addition, the number of serious incidents (physical violence, threat with violence, and defacing of cemeteries and synagogues) decreased by 40 percent. Provisional statistics covering the first 4 months of 2004 confirmed this trend. Reportedly, a considerable number of anti-Semitic offenders were of north-African origin.

Reacting to CIDI reports on increasing anti-Semitism in recent years, the Parliament requested that the Government present an action plan to combat anti-Semitism in June 2003. The Government responded in October 2003 but placed the action plan in the broader context of its efforts to combat discrimination of all kinds, and it did not propose new policy specifically designed to combat anti-Semitism. The plan proposed that parents have primary responsibility for preventing anti-Semitic incidents; however, schools also could help to combat discrimination and inculcate respect and tolerance. Public debate and dialogue were other tools to achieve these goals, and several NGOs launched projects such as Een Ander Joods Geluid (An Alternative Jewish Viewpoint) to foster debate on equality, tolerance, and human dignity. Also, the Dutch Coalition for Peace called on Jews, Palestinians, and other Muslims in the country to work together to restore peace in the Middle East.

Stricter instructions to prosecutors and the police took effect in April 2003 to ensure proper attention to incidents of discrimination. Measures also were taken to deal more effectively with discrimination on the Internet. The Ministry of Education provided schools with guidelines to offer instruction on different religions and ideologies in conjunction with discrimination and intolerance as well as on the persecution of Jewish persons in World War II. The Ministry of Welfare subsidized a special program to teach children about World War II and the persecution of Jewish persons. In particular, the program was designed to raise awareness about the consequences of prejudice. The Government promoted dialogue and supported initiatives to create a better understanding between Jewish persons and Muslims persons.

Norway

Members of the Jewish community reported a doubling of anti-Semitic incidents in the last 2 years. The majority of the roughly 40 reported incidents in 2003 involved verbal harassment of primary and secondary school Jewish students by non-Jewish students. A small number of incidents involved threats against Jewish persons. There were no reports of anti-Semitic violence or vandalism.

The Government was vigilant in fighting anti-Semitism and promoting religious tolerance. In April, Prime Minister Bondevik met with two Norwegian Jewish children who had been harassed on the basis of their religion. At the conclusion of the meeting, he issued a strong public statement condemning anti-Semitism and calling on the public to fight anti-Semitism more actively.

Poland

Surveys over the past several years showed a continuing decline in anti-Semitic sentiment, and avowedly anti-Semitic candidates have won few elections. However, anti-Semitic feelings persisted among certain sectors of the population, occasionally resulting in acts of vandalism and physical or verbal abuse. In prior years, there were reports of sporadic incidents of harassment and violence against Jews and occasional desecration of Jewish cemeteries committed by skinheads and other marginal elements of society.

A credible NGO reported that on October 26 a Jewish youth from Sweden wearing a skullcap while visiting the Auschwitz Extermination Camp encountered three young Poles who shouted anti-Semitic slurs at him. The youth, who reported the incident by e-mail, said that this was not typical of his entire visit to Poland.

In April, the pastor of St. Brigid Church in Gdansk told parishioners during services that "Jews killed Jesus and the prophets" and displayed posters asserting that only Christians could be true citizens. The Archbishop of Gdansk subsequently removed the priest for this and other improprieties.

In June, police in Krakow discovered the desecration of a 19th-century synagogue. Vandals had painted swastikas and a Star of David hanging from gallows on the Temple Synagogue. The desecration occurred a few days before the opening of an International Festival of Jewish Culture in Krakow's Kazimierz district.

In December 2003, a group of Catholics protested what they considered to be anti-Semitic literature sold in a bookstore in the basement of a Warsaw church. The group called for church authorities to close the bookstore, which was run by a private company renting the basement space, and for state authorities to prosecute the bookstore owner for hate crimes. The state prosecutor's office examined the case and found no basis for prosecution. Catholic Church authorities stated that they could not take action due to the bookstore's lease.

The Government supported the American Jewish Committee in establishing a $4 million memorial at the site of the Belzec death camp, where Nazi Germany murdered 500,000 Jews during the Holocaust. Polish President Aleksander Kwasniewski took part in the dedication of the memorial in June.

The Government cooperated with the country's NGOs and officials of major denominations to promote religious tolerance and lend support to activities such as the March of the Living, an event to honor victims of the Holocaust. On April 19, the 13th March of the Living took place. An estimated 6,000 to 7,000 participants, including schoolchildren, Boy Scouts, the Polish-Israeli Friendship Society, Polish survivors of Auschwitz, and the Polish Union of Jewish Students, walked from the former Auschwitz concentration camp to the former Birkenau death camp.

In June, the Government held a major international conference to unveil its proposal to open an international center for human rights education in Oswiecim.

The Government provided grants to a number of organizations involved in anti-bias education, including the public-private Jewish Historical Institute (ZIH) in Warsaw. Many of ZIH's staff were also government employees. ZIH was the largest depository of Jewish-related archival documents, books, journals, and museum objects in the country. The Government also provided grants to the Jewish Historical Association, which produces educational materials on Jewish culture, the Holocaust and religious tolerance, and to other NGOs.

The Institute of National Remembrance - Commission for the Prosecution of Crimes against the Polish Nation (IPN), created by parliament in 1998, is under the direction of a president who acts independently of government control and is elected for a 5-year term. One of the three principal departments of IPN was the Public Education Office, which produces materials for schools, teachers, and students. The office also held competitions, sponsored exhibitions on historical themes, and supported workshops, seminars, and other activities. Educational materials included a major research and documentation project on "The Extermination of Jews in Poland" during World War II. This project included a critical review of attitudes towards the Jewish population during the war, and instances of collaboration with the Nazis, as well as activities undertaken by underground organizations and individuals to rescue Jews.

Local governments have also been active in encouraging tolerance. On December 13, Deputy Mayor of Warsaw Andrzej Urbanski, together with the Chief Rabbi of Israel and Chief Rabbi of Poland, participated in the first public lighting of a Menorah in the history of the Polish capital. Together with Jewish organizations from Poland and abroad, several towns have contributed to the renovation of Jewish cemeteries. Such towns include Ozarow Swietokrzyski, Iwaniska, Goldap, Karczew and Wyszkow.

Romania

The extremist elements of the press continued to publish anti-Semitic articles. The Legionnaires (Iron Guard)--an extreme nationalist, anti-Semitic, pro-Nazi group--continued to republish inflammatory books from the interwar period. A new Iron Guard monthly, Obiectiv Legionar (Legionnaire Focus), carrying mostly old legionnaire literature, began publication in July 2003 and was distributed in several of the largest cities, including Bucharest. The New Right organization (also with legionnaire orientation) continued to sponsor marches and religious services to commemorate Corneliu Zelea Codreanu, the founder of the Legionnaire Movement. Extremists made repeated attempts to deny that Holocaust activities occurred in the country or in territory administered by the country. In March, a private television station broadcast a talk show on "Gypsies, Jews, and Legionnaires," which voiced xenophobic, anti-Semitic, and racist views. The station owners did not respond to a protest sent by the Jewish Communities Federation.

In March, unidentified persons broke into a synagogue in Bacau and broke its windows. The perpetrators were not identified, but were believed to be local youths, rather than members of an organized anti-Semitic movement. In August, Nazi and anti-Semitic signs were found on the inside of the walls of the Jewish cemetery in Sarmasu, Mures County. Five Jewish cemeteries were desecrated in 2003, but no perpetrators were identified in these cases.

On a number of occasions government officials denied or minimized the occurrence of the Holocaust in the country. In July 2003, in an interview with an Israeli newspaper, President Iliescu appeared to minimize the Holocaust by claiming that suffering and persecution were not unique to the Jewish population in Europe. He later said that his interview had been presented in an incomplete and selective way. In December, President Iliescu decorated extremist Greater Romania Party (PRM) leader Corneliu Vadim Tudor with the "Star of Romania," the nation's highest honor. In addition, President Iliescu decorated Gheorghe Buzatu, PRM Vice Chairman and an outspoken Holocaust denier, with the prestigious "Faithful Service" award. This action prompted Elie Wiesel, a Nobel Peace Prize Laureate and Chairman of President Iliescu's International Commission on the Holocaust in Romania, to "resign" from the "National Order of the Star of Romania," and to vow not to wear the decoration that accompanies the award. (Wiesel had received his award in 2002.)

Most mainstream politicians criticized anti-Semitism, racism, and xenophobia publicly. President Iliescu, Prime Minister Adrian Nastase, and several members of the cabinet (the Minister of Foreign Affairs, the Minister of Culture and Religious Denominations, and others) continued to make public statements on various occasions against extremism, anti-Semitism, and xenophobia and criticized attempts to deny the occurrence of the Holocaust in the country. Two government-issued decrees banned fascist, racist, and xenophobic organizations; prohibited the personality cult of war criminals; and protected Jewish cemeteries and synagogues. The Government sponsored several seminars and symposiums on anti-Semitism.

In May, the Government designated October 9 as an annual Holocaust Remembrance Day. On October 9, 1941, the pro-Nazi government of Marshal Antonescu initiated the deportation of thousands of victims from Bessarabia and Bukovina to Transnistria. Senior Government leaders commemorated the first Holocaust Remembrance day by laying wreaths at a Holocaust memorial in the courtyard of a Bucharest synagogue and by holding an ecumenical religious service in the Parliament building.

In May 2003, the Government inaugurated a Holocaust memorial in Targu Mures, a Transylvanian town under Hungarian administration in World War II.

The Government took several steps to improve teaching of the Holocaust in teaching materials and textbooks, although efforts remained limited and inconsistent. In September 2003, the Government released a teaching manual for schools that dealt with Holocaust denial and provided figures for the number of Jews killed and details about concentration camps, death chambers, and the persecution of other groups. History teachers participated in training courses for the teaching of the Holocaust in Paris in 2003 and during the reporting period. Over 50 teachers graduated from the training program at the Holocaust teaching center in Bacau, which was established with the support of the Ministry of Education in 2002.

In October 2003, President Iliescu established the International Commission on the Holocaust in Romania to analyze and to improve public understanding of Holocaust events in the country. The committee, chaired by Elie Wiesel, presented its findings to President Iliescu on November 11, 2004. In addition to fully charting the progression and atrocities of the Romanian

Holocaust, the report contained a list of recommendations for the Romanian Government to ensure that the Holocaust is accurately remembered by the Romanian people. Among the commission's recommendations was that the Romanian Government reverse its rehabilitation of war criminals; open prosecutions for unpunished war crimes; and enforce 2002 legislation making Holocaust denial in Romania a crime.

Russia

An estimated 600,000 to 1 million Jewish persons lived in the country (0.5 percent of the total population) following large-scale emigration during the last 2 decades.

Many in the Jewish community stated that conditions for Jewish persons in the country had improved, primarily because there was no longer any official "state-sponsored" anti-Semitism; however, anti-Semitic incidents against individuals and institutions continued to occur and violence was used during these attacks with increasing frequency. The Anti-Defamation League reported that while the number of anti-Semitic incidents remained stable in 2003, the nature of the attacks became more violent. Anti-Semitic statements were discouraged and have been legally prosecuted. While the Government publicly denounced nationalist ideology and supported legal action against acts of anti-Semitism, reluctance on the part of lower-level officials to call such acts anything other than "hooliganism" remained problematic.

On April 22, eight skinheads stormed the Ulyanovsk Jewish Center screaming, "don't pollute our land," smashing windows, and tearing down Jewish symbols as Jewish women and children hid inside. No one was injured, but police failed to respond quickly, arriving 40 minutes after they were called. A member of the extremist National Bolshevik Party later was arrested in connection with the attack. The investigation was ongoing at year's end, but it was suspected that both events were prompted by the anniversary of Hitler's birthday.

On April 29 in Voronezh, two skinheads attacked Aleksey Kozlov outside the headquarters of the Inter-Regional Human Rights Movement of which he is in charge. Kozlov is the regional monitor for anti-Semitism and racism in the country, a project sponsored by the European Commission.

On October 17, a group of skinheads tried to enter the synagogue in Penza, but were stopped by parishioners. A group of approximately 40 people armed with chains and iron clubs approached the synagogue later that day. The parishioners locked themselves inside and called the police. There were reports that three skinheads were detained.

Unknown persons vandalized Jewish institutions. On many occasions, vandals desecrated tombstones in cemeteries dominated by religious and ethnic minorities. These attacks often involved the painting of swastikas and other racist and ultra-nationalist symbols or epithets on gravestones. On January 27, an explosion shattered several windows in a synagogue in Derbent in the southern region of Dagestan. Vandals attempted to torch a synagogue and library in Chelyabinsk in February, but neighbors managed to extinguish the fire before the arrival of firefighters. Local Jewish community representatives suspected a local anti-Semitic group was responsible for the attack. On March 29, vandals broke the windows of the only kosher restaurant in St. Petersburg. On April 11, a group of young persons threw bottles at a synagogue in Nizhniy Novgorod. The police failed to catch the vandals, and the criminal investigation was dropped on April 22. In September 2003, an anti-Semitic poster with wires attached to it was found at the Velikiy Novgorod Synagogue. There were several attacks on a synagogue in Kostroma. A Jew was injured during an attack in December 2003. Reportedly, teenagers threw stones at the windows and covered the synagogue fence with anti-Semitic inscriptions. Local police doubted they would be able to find the vandals, and a local rabbi said the attack was blamed on hooliganism.

During the reporting period, Jewish cemeteries were desecrated in Bryansk, Kaluga, Kostroma, Petrozavodsk, Pyatigorsk, St. Petersburg, Ulyanovsk, and Vyatka. In Petrozavodsk, unknown persons sprayed anti-Semitic graffiti on tombstones on the day a local court was to render a decision in another case concerning cemetery desecration. In February, several Jewish tombs were desecrated in one of the oldest cemeteries in St. Petersburg; vandals again desecrated Jewish graves there in December. On March 31, a Jewish cemetery was desecrated in Kaluga and, after the local Jewish community chairman notified the governor about the incident, four teenagers and two adults suspected in the vandalism were detained. On November 25, three of the individuals, including one minor, were sentenced to two years probation. The other two participants were too young to be prosecuted. In April, vandals damaged 14 tombstones in Pyatigorsk's Jewish cemetery. In October 2003, a suspected bomb was found on a tomb at the Kostroma Jewish cemetery.

Anti-Semitism and xenophobic thought has become increasingly popular among certain sectors of the population. Nationalistic parties, such as Rodina and the Liberal Democratic Party of Russia (LDPR), gained a wider voter base by addressing issues of nationalism, race, ethnicity, and religion. Allegations of anti-Semitism were leveled at the Rodina bloc, LDPR, and the Communist Party of the Russian Federation (KPRF). Anti-Semitic themes figured in some local election campaigns. There were multiple cases of anti-Semitic statements from government authorities in some of the country's regions, particularly in Krasnodar Kray and Kursk Oblast, as well as in the State Duma.

Originally registered with well-known neo-Nazis on its electoral list, the Rodina bloc attempted to improve its image by rejecting openly neo-Nazi candidates; however, it allowed others known for their anti-Semitic views to remain.

Vladimir Zhirinovskiy and his LDPR party also were known for their anti-Semitic rhetoric and statements. In Moscow during a May Day celebration, LDPR supporters rallied, carrying anti-Semitic signs and spoke out against what they called "world Zionism."

The KPRF also made anti-Semitic statements during the 2003 Duma elections. Krasnodar Kray Senator Nikolai Kondratenko blamed Zionism and Jews in general for many of the country's problems and blamed Soviet Jews for helping to destroy the Soviet Union, according to a November 2003 article in Volgogradskaya Tribuna.

The ultranationalist and anti-Semitic Russian National Unity (RNE) paramilitary organization continued to propagate hostility toward Jews and non-Orthodox Christians. The RNE has lost political influence in some regions since its peak in 1998, but the organization maintained high levels of activity in other regions, such as Voronezh.

Most anti-Semitic crimes were committed by groups of young skinheads. The estimated number of skinheads increased from only a few dozen in 1992 to more than 50,000 in 2004. Typically, skinheads formed loosely organized groups of 10 to 15 persons, and, while these groups did not usually belong to any larger organized structure, they tended to communicate through the hundreds of fascist journals and magazines that exist throughout the country, and increasingly on the Internet.

Many small, radical-nationalist newspapers were distributed throughout the country, sometimes containing anti-Semitic, as well as anti-Muslim and xenophobic leaflets. Anti-Semitic themes continued to figure in some local publications around the country, unchallenged by local authorities. For example, an anti-Semitic novel, The Nameless Beast, by Yevgeny Chebalin, has been on sale in the State Duma's bookstore since September 2003. The xenophobic and anti-Semitic text makes offensive statements about Jews and non-ethnic Russians. According to the Anti-Defamation League, books sold in the Duma were not typically monitored for content. In cases where Jewish or other public organizations attempted to take legal action against the publishers, the courts generally were unwilling to recognize the presence of anti-Semitic content. Some NGOs claimed that many of these publications are owned or managed by the same local authorities that refuse to take action against offenders.

The larger anti-Semitic publications were Russkaya Pravda, Vitaz, and Peresvet, which were available in metro stations around Moscow. In addition, there were at least 80 Russian Web sites dedicated to distributing anti-Semitic propaganda; the law does not restrict Web sites that contain hate speech.

Responses to anti-Semitic violence were mixed. Authorities often provided strong words of condemnation, but preferred to label the perpetrators as terrorists or hooligans rather than xenophobes or anti-Semites. Occasionally, the Government redesignated these events as criminal acts resulting from ethnic hatred. Human rights observers noted that considerable legislation prohibits racist propaganda and racially motivated violence, but complained that it was invoked infrequently. There were some efforts to counter extremist groups during the year.

Federal officials maintained regular contact with Jewish community leaders. In March, then Russian Minister for Nationalities Vladimir Zorin brought extremism to the forefront of public attention by calling anti-Semitism and xenophobia major threats to the country. Zorin called for stricter enforcement of the country's existing statutes outlawing extremism and anti-Semitism and urging tolerance education programs. In addition, Interior Minister Rashid Nurgaliyev became the first high-ranking official to acknowledge the existence of right-wing extremist youth groups in the country and noted combating this extremism was one of the top priority tasks for the Ministry of Internal Affairs and the Federal Security Service. These statements marked a positive step by the Government to prosecute those who commit acts of anti-Semitism, although few concrete steps were taken to solve high-profile cases.

A criminal proceeding was initiated against Boris Mironov, one of the three co-chairs of the National Sovereign Party of Russia, who ran for governor in Novosibirsk. The charges were instigation of national hatred. The major slogan of his election bulletin was "We'll not allow Jews to take power." Experts found the texts of the bulletin anti-Semitic.

In December, Igor Kolodezenko, the publisher of the newspaper Russkiy Sibir, was given a 2 year suspended sentence after being convicted of inciting ethnic hatred for publishing anti-Semitic articles. In June, the Arbitration Court of Sverdlovsk Oblast ordered the shutdown of a local anti-Semitic paper, Russkaya Obshchina Yekaterinburga, after the Court found that the newspaper violated the laws banning incitement of ethnic hatred, according to the Jewish National-Cultural Autonomy of Sverdlovsk Oblast. The newspaper had received three warnings from the Ministry of the Press based on complaints from activists. In 2002, the Prosecutor's office had closed the criminal case. The court also fined a company that published the newspaper approximately $34 (1,000 rubles).

In September, a new course "A History of World Religions" was introduced at some Moscow schools, pursuant to which some students were taken on field trips to local synagogues and other religious institutions to increase mutual understanding. The Government backed away from previous plans to promote a compulsory nationwide course in schools on the "Foundations of Orthodox Culture," using a textbook by that title, which detailed Orthodox Christianity's contribution to the country's culture. Although the book was still used by some schools, the Ministry of Education has rejected funding for another edition and further circulation of the textbook. Many religious minorities had complained about negative language describing non-Orthodox groups, particularly Jewish persons.

In March, prominent rabbis Berl Lazar and Pinchas Goldschmidt together requested that the Government better define the meaning of extremism. Lazar and Goldschmidt said that law enforcement was prone to dismiss anti-Semitic actions as simple hooliganism to avoid calling attention to the presence of extremists in their region, and to consciously protect extremist groups with which they sympathized. In October, President Putin met with Rabbi Lazar and promised that the state would help to revive Jewish communities in Russia.

Serbia and Montenegro

Since July 2003, according to the Forum 18 News Service, more than 50 acts of vandalism on religious property occurred. Many of the attacks involved spray-painted graffiti, rock throwing, or the defacing of tombstones, but a number of cases involved more extensive damage. There were a number of incidents in which gravestones were desecrated, including those in Jewish cemeteries.

Jewish leaders in Serbia reported a continued increase in anti-Semitism on the Internet and the frequent appearance of anti-Semitic hate speech in small-circulation books. The release of new books (or reprints of translations of anti-Semitic foreign literature) often led to an increase in hate mail and other expressions of anti-Semitism. These sources associated anti-Semitism with anti-Western and anti-globalization sentiments, as well as ethnic nationalism.

In 2002, Serbian courts began proceedings in the Savic case, in which an author of anti-Semitic literature was tried for spreading racial or national hatred through the print media. According to sources in the Jewish community, a number of continuances have been issued in this trial. The latest continuance, granted to allow for a psychiatric examination of the defendant, has been ongoing for more than a year.

Slovak Republic

Anti-Semitism persisted among some elements of society and was manifested occasionally in incidences of violence and vandalism.

In early May, sources within the Ministry of the Interior reported that skinheads attacked an Israeli citizen at the main bus station in Bratislava. The man defended himself with a knife and killed his attacker. The police did not release any information to the public about the attack. The Government rarely commented on racially motivated crimes.

In October 2003, the Jewish cemetery in Nove Mesto Nad Vahom was vandalized for the second time, and Jewish leaders reported finding an anti-Semitic poster on a building formerly owned by Jews. The police did not identify the vandals who damaged the 19 gravestones. The text of the poster accused Jews of stealing money received from a government fund for compensation for wartime-confiscated property.

Also in October 2003, three juvenile offenders vandalized the Puchov cemetery in the western part of the country causing $1,613 (50,000 Slovak crowns) in damages and ruining 22 gravestones. The adolescents were given suspended sentences of 4 months to 1 year. Three other individuals under age 15 were not required to stand trial. Investigators did not pursue charges of racial motivation that carried longer sentences because of the lack of physical evidence.

In November 2003, unknown persons desecrated the cemetery in Humenne in the eastern part of the country. Graffiti in German on the entrance gate read "Achtung, Jude" (watch out, Jews) with a swastika below the writing. Swastikas and inscriptions, such as Heil Hitler, Adolf Hitler, and Mein Kampf, appeared on three graves. The Humenne police opened a criminal investigation on charges of supporting movements that suppress the rights of citizens, vandalism, and defamation of peoples, races, and religion. The Humenne cemetery is a national cultural monument, and the damage was irreversible in terms of the tombstones' value. Restoration work in the cemetery had finished just 6 months before the vandalism occurred.

Jewish community leaders praised the quick action of the police in cases of vandalism, but perpetrators usually were minors and received light sentences. The Jewish community successfully pressed for parents of the vandals to pay damages in the 2002 Banovce cemetery case and hoped this case could be successfully replicated.

A Slovak Intelligence Service list of persons allegedly harming the country's interests, which was leaked to the press in mid 2003, identified three individuals as Jewish. The media and politicians criticized the practice of categorizing citizens by religious affiliation.

According to estimates, 500 to 800 neo-Nazis and 3,000 to 5,000 sympathizers operated in the country and committed serious offenses; however, only a small number of these abuses were prosecuted. The Penal Code stipulates that anyone who publicly demonstrates sympathy towards fascism or movements oppressing human rights and freedoms can be sentenced to jail for up to 3 years. Only a small number of these abuses were prosecuted due to court delays.

Some cases were fed by widespread opposition to the Sharon Government and popular support for the Palestinian cause. There have been examples of anti-Semitic graffiti in several large cities. In November, vandals desecrated several graves at a Jewish cemetery in Reggio Emilia, but no anti-Semitic signs or inscriptions were found at the site.

In January, Prime Minister Berlusconi created a new "Inter-Ministerial Commission to Combat Anti-Semitism" to ensure strong, uniform responses to any anti-Semitic acts by the police and government officials. In April, the mayor of Rome announced the establishment of a museum dedicated to the Shoah. In November, the Government created a new office to combat racial and ethnic discrimination through education, mass media campaigns, and judicial assistance to victims of discrimination. The new office lists Muslims, Jews, and foreign workers as the three cultural minorities most likely to face racial or ethnic prejudice in the country. In 2003, the Parliament approved the creation of a National Holocaust Memorial Museum in Ferrara; planning is in process, but construction has not begun. In November 2003, newly appointed Foreign Minister (and Deputy Prime Minister) Gianfranco Fini publicly repudiated his party's Fascist origins, condemned Mussolini's treatment of the Jews, and sought forgiveness during a historic visit to Israel.

The Government hosted meetings to increase educational awareness of the Holocaust and to combat anti-Semitism in Europe.

The country commemorated Holocaust Remembrance Day on January 27. During the reporting period, thousands marched in commemorative processions across the country, several cities staged exhibitions of the 'memory train' used to transport Italian Jews to Nazi concentration camps, and Italian public school students participated in educational and commemorative programs in schools.

With the Foreign Ministry and the Office of the Prime Minister, the Anti-Defamation League hosted a conference on anti-Semitism in Rome in December. Prime Minister Berlusconi, Foreign Minister Fini, and other high-ranking Italian officials participated in the conference.

The Vatican made a serious effort to combat anti-Semitism. The Holy See is active in OSCE endeavors and sent a high-level delegation to the April OSCE anti-Semitism conference in Berlin. A Vatican document released on March 8, instructed bishops on the exercise of their ministry, and implored them to encourage respect for Jews to combat anti-Semitism. It also asked bishops to ensure that the study of Judaism is on the curriculum in their seminaries for priests and to promote dialogue regarding Judaism. The Pope made several statements condemning anti-Semitism. These attracted notice of the Jewish community. For example, Israel's Chief Rabbis expressed thanks to the Pope for his strong condemnation of anti-Semitism during a January 16 audience.

Russia

An estimated 600,000 to 1 million Jewish persons lived in the country (0.5 percent of the total population) following large-scale emigration during the last 2 decades.

Many in the Jewish community stated that conditions for Jewish persons in the country had improved, primarily because there was no longer any official "state-sponsored" anti-Semitism; however, anti-Semitic incidents against individuals and institutions continued to occur and violence was used during these attacks with increasing frequency. The Anti-Defamation League reported that while the number of anti-Semitic incidents remained stable in 2003, the nature of the attacks became more violent. Anti-Semitic statements were discouraged and have been legally prosecuted. While the Government publicly denounced nationalist ideology and supported legal action against acts of anti-Semitism, reluctance on the part of lower-level officials to call such acts anything other than "hooliganism" remained problematic.

On April 22, eight skinheads stormed the Ulyanovsk Jewish Center screaming, "don't pollute our land," smashing windows, and tearing down Jewish symbols as Jewish women and children hid inside. No one was injured, but police failed to respond quickly, arriving 40 minutes after they were called. A member of the extremist National Bolshevik Party later was arrested in connection with the attack. The investigation was ongoing at year's end, but it was suspected that both events were prompted by the anniversary of Hitler's birthday.

On April 29 in Voronezh, two skinheads attacked Aleksey Kozlov outside the headquarters of the Inter-Regional Human Rights Movement of which he is in charge. Kozlov is the regional monitor for anti-Semitism and racism in the country, a project sponsored by the European Commission.

On October 17, a group of skinheads tried to enter the synagogue in Penza, but were stopped by parishioners. A group of approximately 40 people armed with chains and iron clubs approached the synagogue later that day. The parishioners locked themselves inside and called the police. There were reports that three skinheads were detained.

Unknown persons vandalized Jewish institutions. On many occasions, vandals desecrated tombstones in cemeteries dominated by religious and ethnic minorities. These attacks often involved the painting of swastikas and other racist and ultra-nationalist symbols or epithets on gravestones. On January 27, an explosion shattered several windows in a synagogue in Derbent in the southern region of Dagestan. Vandals attempted to torch a synagogue and library in Chelyabinsk in February, but neighbors managed to extinguish the fire before the arrival of firefighters. Local Jewish community representatives suspected a local anti-Semitic group was responsible for the attack. On March 29, vandals broke the windows of the only kosher restaurant in St. Petersburg. On April 11, a group of young persons threw bottles at a synagogue in Nizhniy Novgorod. The police failed to catch the vandals, and the criminal investigation was dropped on April 22. In September 2003, an anti-Semitic poster with wires attached to it was found at the Velikiy Novgorod Synagogue. There were several attacks on a synagogue in Kostroma. A Jew was injured during an attack in December 2003. Reportedly, teenagers threw stones at the windows and covered the synagogue fence with anti-Semitic inscriptions. Local police doubted they would be able to find the vandals, and a local rabbi said the attack was blamed on hooliganism.

During the reporting period, Jewish cemeteries were desecrated in Bryansk, Kaluga, Kostroma, Petrozavodsk, Pyatigorsk, St. Petersburg,

Ulyanovsk, and Vyatka. In Petrozavodsk, unknown persons sprayed anti-Semitic graffiti on tombstones on the day a local court was to render a decision in another case concerning cemetery desecration. In February, several Jewish tombs were desecrated in one of the oldest cemeteries in St. Petersburg; vandals again desecrated Jewish graves there in December. On March 31, a Jewish cemetery was desecrated in Kaluga and, after the local Jewish community chairman notified the governor about the incident, four teenagers and two adults suspected in the vandalism were detained. On November 25, three of the individuals, including one minor, were sentenced to two years probation. The other two participants were too young to be prosecuted. In April, vandals damaged 14 tombstones in Pyatigorsk's Jewish cemetery. In October 2003, a suspected bomb was found on a tomb at the Kostroma Jewish cemetery.

Anti-Semitism and xenophobic thought has become increasingly popular among certain sectors of the population. Nationalistic parties, such as Rodina and the Liberal Democratic Party of Russia (LDPR), gained a wider voter base by addressing issues of nationalism, race, ethnicity, and religion. Allegations of anti-Semitism were leveled at the Rodina bloc, LDPR, and the Communist Party of the Russian Federation (KPRF). Anti-Semitic themes figured in some local election campaigns. There were multiple cases of anti-Semitic statements from government authorities in some of the country's regions, particularly in Krasnodar Kray and Kursk Oblast, as well as in the State Duma.

Originally registered with well-known neo-Nazis on its electoral list, the Rodina bloc attempted to improve its image by rejecting openly neo-Nazi candidates; however, it allowed others known for their anti-Semitic views to remain.

Vladimir Zhirinovskiy and his LDPR party also were known for their anti-Semitic rhetoric and statements. In Moscow during a May Day celebration, LDPR supporters rallied, carrying anti-Semitic signs and spoke out against what they called "world Zionism."

The KPRF also made anti-Semitic statements during the 2003 Duma elections. Krasnodar Kray Senator Nikolai Kondratenko blamed Zionism and Jews in general for many of the country's problems and blamed Soviet Jews for helping to destroy the Soviet Union, according to a November 2003 article in Volgogradskaya Tribuna.

The ultranationalist and anti-Semitic Russian National Unity (RNE) paramilitary organization continued to propagate hostility toward Jews and non-Orthodox Christians. The RNE has lost political influence in some regions since its peak in 1998, but the organization maintained high levels of activity in other regions, such as Voronezh.

Most anti-Semitic crimes were committed by groups of young skinheads. The estimated number of skinheads increased from only a few dozen in 1992 to more than 50,000 in 2004. Typically, skinheads formed loosely organized groups of 10 to 15 persons, and, while these groups did not usually belong to any larger organized structure, they tended to communicate through the hundreds of fascist journals and magazines that exist throughout the country, and increasingly on the Internet.

Many small, radical-nationalist newspapers were distributed throughout the country, sometimes containing anti-Semitic, as well as anti-Muslim and xenophobic leaflets. Anti-Semitic themes continued to figure in some local publications around the country, unchallenged by local authorities. For example, an anti-Semitic novel, The Nameless Beast, by Yevgeny Chebalin, has been on sale in the State Duma's bookstore since September 2003. The xenophobic and anti-Semitic text makes offensive statements about Jews and non-ethnic Russians. According to the Anti-Defamation League, books sold in the Duma were not typically monitored for content. In cases where Jewish or other public organizations attempted to take legal action against the publishers, the courts generally were unwilling to recognize the presence of anti-Semitic content. Some NGOs claimed that many of these publications are owned or managed by the same local authorities that refuse to take action against offenders.

The larger anti-Semitic publications were Russkaya Pravda, Vitaz, and Peresvet, which were available in metro stations around Moscow. In addition, there were at least 80 Russian Web sites dedicated to distributing anti-Semitic propaganda; the law does not restrict Web sites that contain hate speech.

Responses to anti-Semitic violence were mixed. Authorities often provided strong words of condemnation, but preferred to label the perpetrators as terrorists or hooligans rather than xenophobes or anti-Semites. Occasionally, the Government redesignated these events as criminal acts resulting from ethnic hatred. Human rights observers noted that considerable legislation prohibits racist propaganda and racially motivated violence, but complained that it was invoked infrequently. There were some efforts to counter extremist groups during the year.

Federal officials maintained regular contact with Jewish community leaders. In March, then Russian Minister for Nationalities Vladimir Zorin brought extremism to the forefront of public attention by calling anti-Semitism and xenophobia major threats to the country. Zorin called for stricter enforcement of the country's existing statutes outlawing extremism and anti-Semitism and urging tolerance education programs. In addition, Interior Minister Rashid Nurgaliyev became the first high-ranking official to acknowledge the existence of right-wing extremist youth groups in the country and noted combating this extremism was one of the top priority tasks for the Ministry of Internal Affairs and the Federal Security Service. These statements marked a positive step by the Government to prosecute those who commit acts of anti-Semitism, although few concrete steps were taken to solve high-profile cases.

A criminal proceeding was initiated against Boris Mironov, one of the three co-chairs of the National Sovereign Party of Russia, who ran for governor in Novosibirsk. The charges were instigation of national hatred. The major slogan of his election bulletin was "We'll not allow Jews to take power." Experts found the texts of the bulletin anti-Semitic.

In December, Igor Kolodezenko, the publisher of the newspaper Russkiy Sibir, was given a 2 year suspended sentence after being convicted of inciting ethnic hatred for publishing anti-Semitic articles. In June, the Arbitration Court of Sverdlovsk Oblast ordered the shutdown of a local anti-Semitic paper, Russkaya Obshchina Yekaterinburga, after the Court found that the newspaper violated the laws banning incitement of ethnic hatred, according to the Jewish National-Cultural Autonomy of Sverdlovsk Oblast. The newspaper had received three warnings from the Ministry of the Press based on complaints from activists. In 2002, the Prosecutor's office had closed the criminal case. The court also fined a company that published the newspaper approximately $34 (1,000 rubles).

In September, a new course "A History of World Religions" was introduced at some Moscow schools, pursuant to which some students were taken on field trips to local synagogues and other religious institutions to increase mutual understanding. The Government backed away from previous plans to promote a compulsory nationwide course in schools on the "Foundations of Orthodox Culture," using a textbook by that title, which detailed Orthodox Christianity's contribution to the country's culture. Although the book was still used by some schools, the Ministry of Education has rejected funding for another edition and further circulation of the textbook. Many religious minorities had complained about negative language describing non-Orthodox groups, particularly Jewish persons.

In March, prominent rabbis Berl Lazar and Pinchas Goldschmidt together requested that the Government better define the meaning of extremism. Lazar and Goldschmidt said that law enforcement was prone to dismiss anti-Semitic actions as simple hooliganism to avoid calling attention to the presence of extremists in their region, and to consciously protect extremist groups with which they sympathized. In October, President Putin met with Rabbi Lazar and promised that the state would help to revive Jewish communities in Russia.

Serbia and Montenegro

Since July 2003, according to the Forum 18 News Service, more than 50 acts of vandalism on religious property occurred. Many of the attacks involved spray-painted graffiti, rock throwing, or the defacing of tombstones, but a number of cases involved more extensive damage. There were a number of incidents in which gravestones were desecrated, including those in Jewish cemeteries.

Jewish leaders in Serbia reported a continued increase in anti-Semitism on the Internet and the frequent appearance of anti-Semitic hate speech in small-circulation books. The release of new books (or reprints of translations of anti-Semitic foreign literature) often led to an increase in hate mail and other expressions of anti-Semitism. These sources associated anti-Semitism with anti-Western and anti-globalization sentiments, as well as ethnic nationalism.

In 2002, Serbian courts began proceedings in the Savic case, in which an author of anti-Semitic literature was tried for spreading racial or national hatred through the print media. According to sources in the Jewish community, a number of continuances have been issued in this trial. The latest continuance, granted to allow for a psychiatric examination of the defendant, has been ongoing for more than a year.

Slovak Republic

Anti-Semitism persisted among some elements of society and was manifested occasionally in incidences of violence and vandalism.

In early May, sources within the Ministry of the Interior reported that skinheads attacked an Israeli citizen at the main bus station in Bratislava. The man defended himself with a knife and killed his attacker. The police did not release any information to the public about the attack. The Government rarely commented on racially motivated crimes.

In October 2003, the Jewish cemetery in Nove Mesto Nad Vahom was vandalized for the second time, and Jewish leaders reported finding an anti-Semitic poster on a building formerly owned by Jews. The police did not identify the vandals who damaged the 19 gravestones. The text of the poster accused Jews of stealing money received from a government fund for compensation for wartime-confiscated property.

Also in October 2003, three juvenile offenders vandalized the Puchov cemetery in the western part of the country causing $1,613 (50,000 Slovak crowns) in damages and ruining 22 gravestones. The adolescents were given suspended sentences of 4 months to 1 year. Three other individuals under age 15 were not required to stand trial. Investigators did not pursue charges of racial motivation that carried longer sentences because of the lack of physical evidence.

In November 2003, unknown persons desecrated the cemetery in Humenne in the eastern part of the country. Graffiti in German on the entrance gate read "Achtung, Jude" (watch out, Jews) with a swastika below the writing. Swastikas and inscriptions, such as Heil Hitler, Adolf Hitler, and Mein Kampf, appeared on three graves. The Humenne police opened a criminal investigation on charges of supporting movements that suppress the rights of citizens, vandalism, and defamation of peoples, races, and religion. The Humenne cemetery is a national cultural monument, and the damage was irreversible in terms of the tombstones' value. Restoration work in the cemetery had finished just 6 months before the vandalism occurred.

Jewish community leaders praised the quick action of the police in cases of vandalism, but perpetrators usually were minors and received light sentences. The Jewish community successfully pressed for parents of the vandals to pay damages in the 2002 Banovce cemetery case and hoped this case could be successfully replicated.

A Slovak Intelligence Service list of persons allegedly harming the country's interests, which was leaked to the press in mid 2003, identified three individuals as Jewish. The media and politicians criticized the practice of categorizing citizens by religious affiliation.

According to estimates, 500 to 800 neo-Nazis and 3,000 to 5,000 sympathizers operated in the country and committed serious offenses; however, only a small number of these abuses were prosecuted. The Penal Code stipulates that anyone who publicly demonstrates sympathy towards fascism or movements oppressing human rights and freedoms can be sentenced to jail for up to 3 years. Only a small number of these abuses were prosecuted due to court delays.

The low number of prosecutions for racially motivated crime generally improved du The low number of prosecutions for racially motivated crime generally improved durinjournal Personnel, whose editorial board included several parliamentary deputies, generally published one anti-Semitic article each month. The Jewish community received support from public officials in criticizing articles in the journal. On April 20, the State Committee for Nationalities and Migration filed a lawsuit with the Kiev Economic Court to stop publication of Personnel journal and Personnel-Plus newspaper for violation of the Law on Information and the Law on Print Mass Media. On March 12, the State Committee for Nationalities and Migration also filed a lawsuit against Idealist newspaper for publication of anti-Semitic articles.

On January 28, a local court in Kiev ruled that publication of the newspaper Silski Visti be suspended for fomenting interethnic hatred in connection with the 2002 publication of an article by Professor Vasyl Yaremenko entitled "Myth about Ukrainian Anti-Semitism," and a September 2003 article, "Jews in Ukraine: Reality without Myths." Silski Visti viewed the court decision as a government attempt to close the major opposition newspaper (circulation 515,000) prior to the October presidential elections and appealed the ruling. At year's end, Silski Visti's appeal remained under review.

A dispute between nationalists and Jews over the erection of crosses in Jewish cemeteries in Sambir and Kiev remained unresolved, despite mediation efforts by Jewish and Greek Catholic leaders.

A local court ordered a halt in the construction of an apartment building at the site of an old Jewish cemetery in Volodymyr-Volynsky. However, apartment construction was completed during 2003 and most of the units were occupied. Local Jewish groups complained that the State Committee on Religious Affairs continued to refuse to help resolve this dispute.

A large number of high-level government officials continued to take part in the annual September commemoration of the massacre at Babyn Yar in Kiev, the site of one of the most serious crimes of the Holocaust directed against Jews and thousands of individuals from other minority groups. Discussions continued among various Jewish community members about erecting an appropriate memorial, and possibly a heritage center, to commemorate the victims. The Government was generally supportive of these initiatives.

United Kingdom

Anti-Semitic incidents included physical attacks, harassment, desecration of property, vandalism and hateful speech, and racist letters and publications. The Community Security Trust, an organization that analyzed threats to the Jewish community and coordinated with police to provide protection to Jewish community institutions, recorded 511 anti-Semitic incidents between July 2003 and June 2004.

On June 25, near Manchester, a group of five persons physically assaulted a rabbi while shouting anti-Semitic statements. In October 2003, a man driving past Borhamwood Synagogue shouted anti-Semitic statements at members of the synagogue's security team.

The media also reported instances of desecration of synagogues, Jewish cemeteries, and religious texts. On June 17, vandals caused a fire in the South Tottenham United Synagogue that resulted in the destruction of Jewish prayer books smuggled out of Central Europe before World War II. On June 18, in an apparently unrelated incident, a suspicious fire damaged a synagogue and Jewish educational center in Hendon. On August 22, cemetery officials discovered the desecration of approximately 60 gravestones in a Jewish cemetery in Birmingham. Police charged two suspects with racially aggravated criminal damage, racially aggravated public disorder, and causing racially aggravated harassment, alarm, or distress. In November, vandals spray-painted swastikas and other Nazi symbols on 15 gravestones in a Jewish cemetery in Aldershot.

Nazi slogans and swastikas were painted on 11 Jewish gravestones at a Southampton cemetery in July 2003, and 20 Jewish gravestones were damaged at Rainsough cemetery in Manchester in August 2003. Police investigated the attacks as a racist incident. In November 2003, vandals desecrated 21 graves at a Jewish cemetery in Chatham, East Kent. Later in November, a deliberately set fire caused severe damage to the Hillock Hebrew Congregation near Manchester, and, in a separate incident, attackers used bricks to smash the windows of London's Orthodox Edgware Synagogue.

Members of some far-right political parties--such as the BNP, the National Front, and the White Nationalist Party--and some extremist Muslim organizations, such as Al-Muhajiroun, occasionally gave speeches or distributed literature expressing anti-Semitic beliefs, including denials that the Holocaust occurred.

The Crown Prosecution Service advised victims of anti-Semitic attacks on how to report the incidents and press charges against the assailants. Police services investigated anti-Semitic attacks, in addition to providing additional protection to Jewish community events where threat levels were considered to be elevated. The Anti-terrorism, Crime and Security Act of 2001 made it a crime to commit a religiously aggravated offense such as assault, criminal damage, or harassment. The Act also extended the prohibition against incitement to racial hatred to include cases where the hatred was directed at groups located outside the country. In addition, a 2003 regulation explicitly prohibiting racial harassment and a 1980 case law establishing Jews as a racial group provide legal protection against anti-Semitism. Authorities charged 18 persons with religiously aggravated offenses (the religious affiliation of the victims was not released) between December 2001 and March 2003, the most recent period for which data are available; of these, 8 were convicted.

In December 2003, new employment equality regulations regarding religion (or other belief) entered into force. The regulations prohibit employment discrimination based on religious belief, except where there is a "genuine occupational requirement" of a religious nature.

On October 19, police charged Abu Hamza al-Masri with four counts of soliciting or encouraging the killing of Jewish persons based on recordings of some of his addresses to public meetings.

Officials regularly reiterated the government's commitment to addressing anti-Semitism and protecting Jewish citizens through law enforcement and education. In February, Queen Elizabeth II awarded Nazi war crimes investigator Simon Wiesenthal an honorary knighthood in recognition of his efforts to counter anti-Semitism.

The Home Office's Faith Communities Unit ensured that members of all faiths enjoyed the same life opportunities. The unit also sponsored projects that encourage dialogue and cooperation between the different faith communities represented in the country. The Home Office also was responsible for an annual Holocaust Memorial Day.

All publicly maintained schools were required to teach religious tolerance. On October 28, Education and Skills Secretary Charles Clarke introduced a new national framework for schools to deliver religious education that, among other things, teach pupils about others' religious faiths.

Uzbekistan

Anti-Semitic fliers signed by Hizb ut-Tahrir have been distributed throughout the country; however, these views were not representative of the feelings of the vast majority of the population.

Jews generally are able to practice their religion in Uzbekistan, and there were no reports of verbal harassment, physical abuse, or desecration of monuments or cemeteries related to anti-Semitism. Respected Jewish community members report they feel very welcome in the country.

The Government of Uzbekistan promotes anti-bias and tolerance education in its eleventh grade history textbooks. The standardized textbook teaches students about the horrors of the Holocaust, the Nazis' anti-Semitic policy, extermination camps, and the number of Jews killed. In addition, Jewish organizations regularly conduct seminars on Holocaust and anti-Semitism awareness.

Anti-Semitism in the Near East and North Africa Region

Society and legislation in nations in the region, except for Israel and Lebanon, reflect the views of an overwhelmingly Muslim population and a strong Islamic tradition. At times, both social behavior and legislation discriminated against members of minority religions. Government efforts to limit or reprimand anti-Semitic expressions have been infrequent, and governments in the region generally have made only minimal efforts to promote anti-bias and tolerance education.

Anti-Semitic violence was almost entirely associated with anti-Israeli terrorism and was not geographically widespread. Numerous attacks occurred in Israel and in the Occupied Territories, and incitements to violence originated from the Occupied Territories. As well, terrorist bombings in Morocco in May 2003 and at the Taba Hilton in Egypt in October were accompanied by communiques containing anti-Semitic as well as anti-Israeli statements. Terrorist organizations' propaganda in the region frequently was anti-Semitic, as well as anti-Israeli.

Anti-Israeli sentiment linked to the Palestinian question was widespread throughout the Arab population in the region and incorporated anti-Semitic stereotypes in the print and electronic media, public discourse, religious sermons, and the educational system. Additionally, there were some restrictions on Jewish citizens' ability to participate in political life in Syria and Yemen.

Anti-Semitism in the media was the most common form of anti-Semitism in the region. Anti-Semitic articles and opinion pieces, usually rhetoric by political columnists, were published, and editorial cartoons depicted demonic images of Jews and Israeli leaders, stereotypical images of Jews along with Jewish symbols, and comparisons of Israeli leaders to Hitler and the Nazis. These expressions occurred in certain publications and were not common, but they did occur without Government response in Bahrain, Jordan, Kuwait, Oman, Qatar, and the United Arab Emirates. Anti-Semitic articles appeared periodically in the Algerian press without Government response. Apart from Israel and the settlements in the Occupied Territories, the Jewish population in the region is very small. Most of the Jewish population that previously lived in the region has migrated to Israel, Europe, and North America. The "American Jewish

Yearbook 2004" estimated the Jewish population in the region to have been: Israel 4,880,000; West Bank and Gaza 220,000; Iran 11,000; Morocco 5,500; Tunisia 1,500; Yemen 200; Egypt 100; and Syria 100.

Egypt

Anti-Semitic articles and opinion pieces in the print media and editorial cartoons appeared in the press and electronic media. For example, on March 18, Abdelwahab Ads, deputy editor of Al Jumhuriya, accused the Jews of the terrorist attack in Madrid on March 11 as well as of the September 11, 2001, attacks.

On June 24 and July 1, the National Democratic Party (NDP) newspaper al-Lewa al-Islami published articles by Professor Refaat Sayed Ahmed in which he denied the Holocaust. On August 25, the NDP announced that it had banned Professor Ahmed from future publishing, that the editor who approved his article had been fired, and that the NDP and the Government rejected anti-Semitism and acknowledged the reality of the Holocaust.

The Government reportedly has advised journalists and cartoonists to avoid anti-Semitism. Government officials insisted that anti-Semitic statements in the media are a reaction to Israeli government actions against Palestinians and do not reflect historical anti-Semitism; however, there are relatively few public attempts to distinguish between anti-Semitism and anti-Israeli sentiment.

On January 5, the Supreme Administrative Court upheld a 2001 lower court decision to cancel the Abu Hasira festival (for Jewish pilgrims) in the Beheira Governorate. In 2003, the Ministry of Culture had designated Abu Hasira's tomb as a "historic site" and ruled that an annual festival could be held. Villagers around the shrine protested, claiming that the Jewish visitors aggravated the locals with their drinking.

In December 2003, following international expressions of concern, the special collections section of the Alexandria Library removed a copy of "The Protocols of the Elders of Zion" from a display of religious manuscripts. In a statement, the director of the library denied allegations that the book had been displayed next to the Torah, but nonetheless stated that its inclusion was a "bad judgment" and regretted any offense the incident might have caused.

Iran

According to some NGOs, the media contained anti-Semitic content, including articles and editorial cartoons. Although Jews are a recognized religious minority with a reserved seat in parliament (the Majlis), allegations of official discrimination were frequent. The Government's anti-Israeli policies, along with a perception among radical Muslims that all Jewish citizens support Zionism and Israel, created a hostile atmosphere for the 11,000-member community. For example, many newspapers celebrated the 100th anniversary of the publication of the anti-Semitic "The Protocols of the Elders of Zion." Recent demonstrations have included the denunciation of "Jews," as opposed to the past practice of denouncing only "Israel" and "Zionism," adding to the threatening atmosphere for the community.

The Government reportedly allowed Hebrew instruction; however, it strongly discouraged the distribution of Hebrew texts, which made it difficult to teach the language. Jewish citizens were permitted to obtain passports and to travel outside the country, but they often were denied the multiple-exit permits normally issued to other citizens. With the exception of certain business travelers, the authorities required Jewish persons to obtain clearance and pay additional fees before each trip abroad. The Government appeared concerned about the emigration of Jewish citizens, and permission generally was not granted for all members of a Jewish family to travel outside the country at the same time. Jewish leaders reportedly were reluctant to draw attention to official mistreatment of their community due to fear of government reprisal.

Iraq

After the promulgation of the Transitional Administrative Law in February, the former Governing Council addressed the question of whether Jewish expatriates would be allowed to vote in the 2005 elections. It announced that they would be treated like any other expatriate group. The Government has also denied unfounded rumors (sometimes spread in flyers distributed by antigovernment extremist groups) that Jewish expatriates were buying up real estate in an attempt to reassert their influence in the country.

Israel

Palestinian terrorist organizations, including Hamas, Palestinian Islamic Jihad, and the Al Aqsa Martyrs Brigades attacked Israelis and sometimes issued anti-Semitic statements following their attacks.

The Government has actively sought to enlist the international community, including international organizations, to address anti-Semitism. Government officials routinely traveled to other countries to discuss perceived problems of anti-Semitism in those countries. Several local NGOs were dedicated to promoting tolerance and religious co-existence. Their programs included events to increase Jewish-Arab dialogue and cooperation.

Lebanon

Religious tolerance was integral to the country's political system; however, the Arab-Israeli conflict and Israel's occupation of South Lebanon nurtured a strong antipathy toward Israelis, and Lebanese media often reflected that sentiment. Hizballah, through its media outlets, regularly directed strong rhetoric against Israel and its Jewish population and characterized events in the region as part of a "Zionist conspiracy."

The TV series, Ash-Shatat ("The Diaspora"), which centered on the alleged conspiracy of the "The Protocols of the Elders of Zion" to dominate the world, was aired in October and November 2003 by the Lebanon-based satellite television network Al-Manar, which is owned by the terrorist organization Hizballah.

Morocco

Representatives of the centuries-old Jewish minority generally lived throughout the country in safety; however, in September 2003, a Jewish merchant was murdered in an apparently religiously motivated killing. During the May 2003 terrorist attacks, members of the Salafiya Jihadia targeted a Jewish community center in Casablanca. After the attacks, Muslims marched in solidarity with Jews to condemn terrorism. There have been thousands of arrests and many prosecutions of persons tied to the May bombing and other extremist activity. Annual Jewish commemorations normally took place around the country, and Jewish pilgrims from around the region regularly came to holy sites in the country. The Government actively promoted tolerance. Government officials and private citizens often cited the country's tradition of religious tolerance as one of its strengths.

Occupied Territories

Palestinian terrorist groups carried out attacks against Israeli civilians. While these attacks were usually carried out in the name of Palestinian nationalism, the rhetoric used by these organizations sometimes included expressions of anti-Semitism.

The rhetoric of some Muslim religious leaders at times constituted an incitement to violence or hatred. For example, the television station controlled by the Palestinian Authority broadcast statements by Palestinian political and spiritual leaders that resembled traditional expressions of anti-Semitism.

In a sign of positive change, the Friday sermon of December 3, broadcast on Palestinian Authority Television, preacher Muhammad Jammal Abu Hunud called for the development of a modern Islamic discourse, to recognize the "other," to treat him with tolerance, and to avoid extremism and violence.

Saudi Arabia

There were frequent instances in which mosque preachers, whose salaries are paid by the Government, used strongly anti-Jewish language in their sermons. Although this language declined in frequency since the May 2003 attacks in Riyadh, there continued to be instances in which mosque speakers prayed for the death of Jews, including from the Grand Mosque in Mecca and the Prophet's Mosque in Medina.

Anti-Semitic sentiments, ranging from statements by senior officials to editorial cartoons, were present in the print and electronic media. The local press rarely printed articles or commentaries disparaging other religions.

NGOs have reported on intolerance in the Saudi education system, and in particular the presence of anti-Semitic content in some school textbooks.

Saudi authorities have taken measures to address these concerns, including in 2003 the wholesale review of textbooks to remove content disparaging religions other than Islam.

The official Saudi tourism website previously contained a ban on the entry of Jews among others into the Kingdom; on March 1, the Government removed this ban from the site replacing it with a statement regretting "any inconvenience this may have caused."

Syria

The Government barred Jewish citizens from government employment and exempted them from military service obligations, due to tense relations with Israel. Jews also were the only religious minority group whose passports and identity cards noted their religion. Jewish citizens must obtain permission from the security services before traveling abroad and must submit a list of possessions to ensure their return to the country. Jews also faced extra scrutiny from the Government when applying for licenses, deeds, or other government papers. The Government applied a law against exporting any of the country's historical and cultural treasures to prohibit the Jewish community from sending historical Torahs abroad.

Several NGOs reported that the press and electronic media contained anti-Semitic material. A Syrian production company created a TV series, Ash-Shatat ("The Diaspora"), an anti-Semitic program, and filmed it inside the country. The theme of this program centered on the alleged conspiracy of the "Elders of Zion" to orchestrate both world wars and manipulate world markets to create Israel. The show was not aired in the country, but it was shown elsewhere. The closing credits of the programs give "special thanks" to various government ministries, including the security ministry, the culture ministry, the Damascus Police Command, and the Department of Antiquities and Museums.

There were occasional reports of friction between religious faiths, which could be related to deteriorating economic conditions and internal political issues. For example, in 2003, there were reports of minor incidents of harassment and property damage against Jews in Damascus perpetrated by persons not associated with the Government. According to local sources, these incidents were in reaction to Israeli actions against Palestinians.

Tunisia

Since 1999, the Government has not permitted registration of a Jewish religious organization in Djerba; however, the organization performed religious activities and charitable work unhindered. There were unconfirmed reports of a few incidents of vandalism directed against the property of members of the Jewish community. The Government took a wide range of security measures to protect synagogues, particularly during Jewish holidays, and Jewish community leaders said that the level of protection that the Government provided increased during the reporting period. Government officials and private citizens often cited the country's tradition of religious tolerance as one of its strengths.

United Arab Emirates

In August 2003, the Government closed the Zayed Centre for Coordination and Follow-up, a local think tank that published and distributed literature, sponsored lectures, and operated a website. The center published some materials with anti-Jewish themes, and hosted some speakers who promoted anti-Jewish views. The Government stated that it closed the center because its activities "starkly contradicted the principles of interfaith tolerance" advocated by the president.

Yemen

In June, the Government issued a press release accusing Jews in northern Yemen of backing a rebellion in Sa'da; however, the Government shortly thereafter retracted the statement. The media was prone to conspiracy stories involving Jews and Israel. After the ruling party tried to put forward a Jewish candidate, the General Election Committee adopted a policy barring all non-Muslims from running for Parliament.

Anti-Semitism in the Western Hemisphere

Overall, anti-Semitism was not a widespread problem in the Western Hemisphere. Countries such as Brazil, Uruguay, Colombia, and Bolivia reported isolated acts of anti-Semitic graffiti and anti-Semitic material on Internet sites, mostly by small neo-Nazi and skinhead organizations. Authorities in these countries investigated anti-Semitic incidents and prosecuted responsible parties.

Anti-Semitism remained a problem in Argentina. The number of reported anti-Semitic incidents has stabilized in recent years, although there was an increase in documented reports towards the end of the year. NGOs continued to report vandalism of several Jewish cemeteries, threats to Jewish institutions, sales of Nazi memorabilia, graffiti, and display of Nazi symbols. Authorities continued investigations of anti-Semitic acts and launched public efforts to promote interethnic and interreligious understanding.

Canada experienced an increasing number of anti-Semitic incidents in recent years, including a school bombing, physical violence, and vandalism of synagogues, schools, cemeteries, and private houses in predominantly Jewish neighborhoods. B'nai B'rith Canada estimated 600 cases of anti-Semitism during the first 8 months of the year.

Argentina

There have been a number of recent anti-Semitic incidents. Notable incidents during the reporting period included vandalism of Jewish cemeteries (including the Israeli Cemetery of Ciudadela on the outskirts of Buenos Aires that was vandalized on several occasions), numerous anti-Semitic remarks, threats to Jewish institutions, sales of Nazi memorabilia, and graffiti and display of Nazi symbols (including a school bus belonging to a Jewish school defaced with Nazi symbols in November). In 2003, the Delegation of Israeli Argentine Associations (DAIA) Center for Social Studies reported 177 anti-Semitic incidents. DAIA had not compiled final figures for the year, but expected to report a similar number of incidents as 2003. The DAIA noted that anti-Semitic incidents made up 7 percent of the complaints received by the National Institute Against Discrimination, Xenophobia, and Racism (INADI) in 2003.

A City of Buenos Aires legislator came under considerable attack following accusations that she made anti-Semitic remarks to a city employee who she subsequently fired. The city legislature investigated the case, and the legislator admitted the facts and publicly apologized, but the legislature was unable to obtain the necessary votes to sanction officially the legislator. INADI issued its determination that the city legislator had committed "ethnic-religious discrimination" under the provisions of the 1988 Federal Anti-discrimination Act and will submit its finding to the city legislature, which may take up the case again in its next session.

There were no developments in the investigations of the January 2002 desecration of a Jewish cemetery in the Buenos Aires suburb of Berazategui, the April 2001 letter bomb received by Alberto Merenson, or in other open cases. The Government also reported that there were no developments in the investigation of the 1992 bombing of the Israeli Embassy. The investigation into the 1994 bombing of the AMIA cultural center, which killed 86 people, resulted in the issuance of international arrest warrants for 12 Iranian officials and a Lebanese national associated with Hizballah. In September, a 3-judge panel acquitted 22 Argentinean defendants charged in connection with the bombing, but the Argentine Government has pledged to continue the investigation and efforts to bring the perpetrators to justice.

Brazil

There were isolated reports of anti-Semitism, and there were signs of increasing tension between Jewish and Muslim citizens. Leaders in the Jewish community expressed concern over the continued appearance of anti-Semitic material on Internet websites compiled by neo-Nazi and "skinhead" groups. There were no reports of violent incidents directed at Jews during the reporting period, although there were reports of anti-Semitic graffiti at synagogues, Jewish cemeteries, and Jewish community centers in Campinas, Curitiba, and Recife. There also were reports of harassment, vandalism, and several anonymous bomb threats and threats of violence via telephone and e-mail during the reporting period. In September 2003, the Supreme Court upheld a 1996 Rio Grande do Sul state court conviction for racism of editor Siegfried Ellwanger, who edited and wrote anti-Semitic books. The lower court's ruling sentenced Ellwanger to a prison term of 2 years, although this sentence subsequently was converted to community service.

Canada

According to the League for Human Rights of B'nai B'rith, the number of anti-Semitic incidents has been steadily increasing over the last decade, with the number of reports doubling from 2001 to 2003. B'nai B'rith reported that there were 600 incidents of anti-Semitism during the first 8 months of the year, surpassing the total reported during 2003.

During the reporting period, there were several acts of anti-Semitism at schools, including the firebombing of a Jewish school in Montreal in April and several incidents of hate speech at Ryerson University in Toronto. In May, authorities arrested three persons in connection with the firebombing, including two 18-year-old youths, and charged them with arson and conspiracy. There were also numerous reports of vandalism at Jewish schools, cemeteries, and synagogues during the reporting period. In June, vandals toppled more than 20 gravestones in the historic Beth Israel cemetery in Quebec City, a designated national historic site.

Senior government officials, including the Prime Minister, have acknowledged that violence directed against the Jewish community was a growing problem and condemned anti-Semitic acts when they have occurred.

Mexico

During the reporting period, the country's Jewish community did not encounter violence, harassment, or vandalism. There were occasional protests associated with the ongoing turmoil in the Middle East, but the Government acted quickly to offer protection. In 2003, both houses of Congress unanimously passed the Federal Law for Preventing and Eliminating Discrimination. The law's fourth article explicitly mentions anti-Semitism as a form of discrimination.

Uruguay

In April, anti-Semitic and pro-Nazi statements were painted in and around Jewish cemeteries. The graffiti was quickly painted over by authorities, although no arrests were made. In 2002, a limited outbreak of anti-Semitic graffiti and propaganda received media attention. Several citizens, including a former minister, were defamed in the graffiti, and there were reports of harassment by telephone. In response, the police arrested three juvenile "skinheads" and confiscated their weapons. The adolescents were indicted and were awaiting trial at year's end.

Venezuela

Statements by senior government officials supporting Iraq's Saddam Hussein and Islamic extremist movements raised tensions and intimidated the country's Jewish community. There were several reports of anti-Semitic graffiti at synagogues in Caracas and two reported threatening phone calls made to Jewish community centers. In August, President Chavez cautioned citizens against following the lead of Jewish citizens in the effort to overturn his referendum victory. Anti-Semitic leaflets also were available to the public in an Interior and Justice Ministry office waiting room.

In November, the Venezuelan Investigative Police searched the Jewish Day School in Caracas, claiming to have reports of weapons cached on the school grounds. According to media reports, rumors of an Israeli connection to the assassination of a Venezuelan federal prosecutor prompted the search. (The federal judge who issued the search warrant was also leading the investigation into the prosecutor's death.) The police found nothing, but their 3-hour search disrupted the school day and alarmed parents. Leaders of the Jewish community expressed outrage following the incident.

Anti-Semitism in East Asia and the Pacific

Anti-Semitism was not a widespread problem in East Asian Pacific countries, where Jewish communities were small. There were overt anti-Semitic incidents in Australia and New Zealand where the communities were somewhat larger.

Australia

The Federal Parliament and most state and territory legislatures passed motions condemning racism against the Jewish community following publication of an Executive Council of Australian Jewry report that noted a continuing, significant level of anti-Semitic attacks. There was a small decrease in anti-Semitic incidents in Australia this year compared to 2003, in contrast to the gradual increase seen in recent years. On January 5, anti-Semitic slogans were burned into the lawns of the Parliament House in the state of Tasmania. Between February and July, several Asian businesses and a synagogue in Western Australia's capital city of Perth were firebombed or sprayed with racist graffiti. In August, a Perth court convicted three men, two of whom were associated with the Australian Nationalist Movement, a Neo-Nazi group, for their roles in the attacks. The ANM members were sentenced to jail for periods of 7 and 10 months.

New Zealand

In August and September, headstones of Jewish graves were smashed or desecrated in two cemeteries in and around Wellington and Wanganui, and a Jewish prayer house was burned in the Wellington area. The Government condemned these actions, and an investigation was ongoing at year's end. The heads of the city's Muslim and Jewish communities said that they believed anti-Semitic and anti-Muslim attacks there were the work of someone outside their communities who wished to incite racial tension between them. The Human Rights Commission, which is Government funded, actively promoted tolerance and anti-bias on the issue.

Malaysia

In an October 2003 speech to the summit of the Organization of the Islamic Conference in the country, then-Prime Minister Mahathir Mohamad said that, "Jews ruled this world by proxy." Prime Minister Abdullah Badawi, who succeeded Mahathir 2 weeks after the speech, subsequently emphasized religious tolerance towards all faiths. During the period, the Government promoted Islam "Hadhari", which emphasized tolerance towards other religions and a moderate, progressive interpretation of Islam.

Anti-Semitism in South Asia

Anti-Semitism is not an issue of any significance in India, nor in the smaller South Asian countries, specifically Bangladesh, Afghanistan, Sri Lanka, Maldives, Nepal, and Bhutan.

Pakistan

Although there are very few Jewish citizens in the country, anti-Semitic press articles are common in the vernacular press. NGO sources point out that since India's 1992 establishment of diplomatic relations with Israel, the Pakistani media, both mainstream and Islamic, sometimes refers to India as the "Zionist threat on our borders." Nonetheless, the attitude of the media is not reflected in the actions of the Government. The Government cooperated in the capture of those responsible for the 2002 abduction and killing of Wall Street Journal Correspondent Daniel Pearl.

Anti-Semitism in Africa

With the exception of the occasional report of an anti-Semitic article appearing in newspapers, anti-Semitism in general was not a problem throughout sub-Saharan Africa. There are very small Jewish populations in most African countries, and embassy reports overwhelmingly indicate that they do not face problems. The vast majority of governments generally respect religious freedom.

South Africa

South Africa has largest populations of Jews on the continent with an estimated 80,000. While there were occasional reports of desecration and vandalism or verbal or written harassment, no violent incidents were noted during the reporting period.

End government report.

The above epilogue chronicled the state of world-wide anti-Semitism from 2000A.D. to approximately 2005. As of this writing in 2016 and 2017 the curse of anti-Semitism has gotten worse. "We are not anti-Semites; we only desire the eradication of the Jewish State of Israel." This is double talk. Even Pope Francis has stated that, "To attack Jews is anti-Semitism, but an outright attack on the State of Israel is also anti-Semitism. There may be political disagreements between governments and on political issues, but the State of Israel has every right to exist in safety and prosperity."

Whereas anti-Semitism had always been a right wing phenomenon, it also started involving young left wingers as they surf the web, learn in universities, and listen to the United Nations where anti-Semitic thought has been proliferating.

After 4,000 years, there is no end in sight for the world's longest hatred.

In two recent studies, less than half of participants in an ADL global poll have heard of the Holocaust; and the Palestinian Authority was deemed to be the most anti-Semitic territory on earth.

Let us all pray that there will never be a repeat of the horrors of the 1940's when world-wide conditions promoted the rise of a narcissistic fanatic who managed to successfully kill 6,000,000 Jews and 54,000,000 non-Jews.

THE END

Printed in the United States
By Bookmasters